A READABLE FEAST

A READABLE FEAST

Sweet, Funny, and Strange
Tales for Every Taste

Edited by

A. E. Decker, Marianne H. Donley, and Carol L. Wright

BETHLEHEM WRITERS GROUP, LLC
BETHLEHEM, PENNSYLVANIA

A
READABLE
FEAST

The contents of this volume are works of fiction. All characters, organizations, and events portrayed are either products of the author's imagination or are used fictitiously.

First edition: November 2015
ISBN: 978-0-9892650-2-7
Library of Congress Control Number applied for
Printed in the United States of America

Cover Image and Design © 2015 Marianne H. Donley
Interior Design and Layout by Melanie Powell, Shybuck Studios

To our faithful readers who have supported us,
and to our future readers who inspire us.

Also from the Bethlehem Writers Group

A Christmas Sampler
Sweet, Funny, and Strange Holiday Tales
Winner of 2010 Next Generation Indie Book Awards
Best Short Fiction and *Best Anthology*

Once Around the Sun
Sweet, Funny, and Strange Tales for All Seasons
Finalist, 2014 Next Generation Indie Book Awards
Best Anthology

Let It Snow
The Best of Bethlehem Writers Roundtable
Winter 2015 Collection

Bethlehem Writers Roundtable
Literary Journal of the Bethlehem Writers Group
http://bwgwritersroundtable.com

Bethlehem Writers Roundtable
Annual Short Story Award
For more information see
http://bwgwritersroundtable.com

The Bethlehem Writers Daily
paper.li/BethlehemWriter/1325670670

The Daily Wryter
paper.li/BettysTips/1325667986

The Bethlehem Writers Group is a community of mutually supportive fiction and non-fiction authors based in Bethlehem, Pennsylvania. The members are as different from each other as their stories, spanning a range of genres including: children's, fantasy, humor, inspirational, literary fiction, memoir, mystery, paranormal, romance, science fiction, women's fiction, and young adult. They meet regularly to help each other refine their craft. Learn more at their website: bethlehemwritersgroup.com.

TABLE OF CONTENTS

Rightful Prey *3*
  A.E. Decker

Early Birds *11*
  Paul Weidknecht

Breakfast for One *19*
  Geoffrey Mehl

Bump and Run *21*
  Diane Sismour

Hard Times *39*
  Jerry McFadden

Sweet Tooth *43*
  Ralph Hieb

Nana's Vegetable Soup *51*
  Carol L. Wright

Twenty-one Greens *57*
  Judith Mehl

Marmalade *63*
  Headley Hauser

The Widow Next Door *67*
  Marianne H. Donley

Preserves *81*
TRACY FALENWOLFE
Winner of the 2014 Bethlehem Writers Roundtable Short Story Award

Metempsychosis *87*
BERNADETTE DE COURCEY

Broken Heart Cakes *93*
TERRIE DAUGHERTY

Bowled Over *99*
COURTNEY ANNICCHIARICO

Natures of Origin *103*
DIANE SISMOUR

How Sweet It Is *111*
A. E. DECKER

The History of a Fruitcake *127*
C. A. ROWLAND
Winner of the 2015 Bethlehem Writers Roundtable Short Story Award

Bacon *135*
HEADLEY HAUSER

Our Town is Different *139*
SALLY PARADYSZ

Cake *157*
E.L. RYAN

The Hunt *163*
CAROL L. WRIGHT

The Pickle Promenade *165*
    JEFF BAIRD

Nectar of the Gods *169*
    RALPH HIEB

Recipe for Disaster *177*
    A.E. DECKER

The King's Potatoes *183*
    JERRY MCFADDEN

As Dawn Brightens. *189*
    PAUL WEIDKNECHT

Chicken Flautas *193*
    EMILY P. W. MURPHY

About the Authors 207

Acknowledgements 212

Rightful Prey

A. E. Decker

The sun was dipping below the horizon when the villagers arrived with dinner.

About time, thought the dragon. His stomach growled as the sounds of struggling filtered into his den. He hoped this one was juicier. Call him suspicious, but he believed their last offering might have been a nun. The book she'd whacked him with before he swallowed her had certainly been black and thick enough to be a Bible. Given him gas, too.

Rock scraped earth as the great stone half-covering the entrance to his lair was heaved aside. Sounds of struggling grew clearer. Through the gap, the dragon caught glimpses of thrashing limbs—young, firm, pink limbs. He smacked his chops.

"Let go of me!" cried a not-quite dulcet voice. An instant later, a bundle of skirts, hair, and apple cheeks came stumbling through the opening, as if propelled by a hearty shove.

"Eep," cried the girl, tripping over a spur of rock and sprawling across the cave's floor. As she sat up, the entrance stone crunched back into place, a noise quickly followed by the patter of footsteps beating a hasty retreat.

"Bastards," muttered the girl, brushing off her clothes.

The dragon ran a gourmet's eye over her. The latest dish on his menu was a tall, hearty, farm-girl type. Instead of the almost requisite fiery red locks, she sported a crown of soft wheaten curls. Her eyes were big and round, but he didn't quite like the way they squinted, probing the cave's depths. They narrowed further when they fell on him.

Ah, well, he judged girls on flavor and crunch, not appearance. "Hello, my dear," he said, using the soft, suave tone he'd deliberately calculated. Terrified prey tasted bitter and astringent.

"Wonderful," the girl muttered. "The big lizard talks." She shook out her voluminous skirts. Something jangled, and the dragon recalled some village girls sewed bells to their petticoats for festive occasions. He made a mental note to chew carefully lest one stick in his throat.

"Won't you come closer, so we might converse?" he said, forgiving her the "big lizard" comment. Only natural she'd feel aggrieved, considering the circumstances.

The girl snorted. "Closer to your teeth, you mean? No thanks."

A wisp of smoke escaped the dragon's nostrils along with a sigh. "Let's be rational about your situation." He aimed a jet of fire towards a jumble of logs arranged in a dimple in the cavern floor—he occasionally liked to watch his jade-green scales glitter in the firelight. The old wood ignited instantly. The flames threw dancing shadows off the irregular rocky walls and colorful sparks off his gemstone nest.

"Oh," said the girl in a small voice as the yellow glow also revealed his vast bulk, filling two-thirds of the cave. Nowhere to run. Some girls tried, of course. He hated that. Adrenalin turned their flesh sour, and often, in catching them, he accidentally crushed them against the floor or a rocky wall. He disliked the texture of pâté.

The girl glanced back towards the entrance. "You're not strong enough to move that rock by yourself," said the dragon, interpreting her gaze. "It takes three men from the village, one of them that brute Wilhelm, whose shoulders resemble a pair of oxen perched to either side of his head."

The girl's gaze returned to him. Her lip quivered.

"Come sit by me," said the dragon, adding even more oil and silk to his tone. He patted a smooth, cupped stone near the fire pit. "I have a bottle of wine. We'll talk, and you may drink as much as you like." *Hopefully enough to cause her to doze off,* he thought. Not only would she be all relaxed and tender then, but he'd enjoy the faint, alcoholic bite the drink would impart to her meat.

All right, he was something of an epicure.

She hesitated an instant longer, then advanced, clearly wary of the dark plumes of smoke drifting from his nostrils. Probably afraid he'd cut loose with the flames the instant she was within range. He almost told her she needn't worry, that he preferred the delectable juiciness of raw prey—but realized in time that she wouldn't find such information reassuring. She sat on the smooth stone with a faint jangle of skirts and held her palms to the flames.

"This is nice, isn't it?" said the dragon encouragingly, a minute or so after she'd settled. His long neck dipped to fish out the bottle of wine from under the knight skeleton in the corner. He dropped it in the girl's lap. "Help yourself to any of the goblets," he said, indicating his twinkling bedding.

She chose a golden one, ornamented with moonstones. She poured a trickle of red wine into it, took a sip, then lowered it stiffly into her lap.

"What's your name?" asked the dragon, hoping a nice chat might relax her. At least she'd see she wasn't about to be devoured by some thug.

"Antonia," she said, staring into the flames.

That was encouraging. He'd thought she might be the sort to mope, ask: "What does it matter?" making for an awkward round of conversation.

"You live on a farm, don't you?" he asked.

"Yes." Her head tilted. "How'd you know that?"

"I can smell animals and tilled earth on your clothes," he

said, tapping his snout with a claw. "My sense of smell is quite amazing."

"Oh, I see." She took another sip of wine. "Is that how you can tell I'm suitable?"

The question threw him. "Suitable?"

"For . . . you know." She made exaggerated chewing motions.

"Oh, that." He'd been trying to steer the conversation away from his forthcoming meal. "No."

"Wait a minute." Antonia leaned forward with another jingle, the wine slopping dangerously in her goblet. "You do only eat maidens, don't you?"

"Of course." The dragon's wings curled at the thought of consuming used flesh.

"So if it's not by smell, how can you tell if a girl's a maiden?"

The dragon paused. "I just . . . know?" His pointed ears twitched. Funny. He'd never thought about it before.

Antonia scoffed. The dragon shot a look at her "What?"

"Nothing." She swirled wine in her goblet. "It's just that you sounded like, well, so like a boy there. They always think they know."

Her eyes had that narrow, calculating look about them again. The hint of a smirk played about her lips.

"What is that supposed to mean?"

"What do you think it means?" She lifted the goblet. He thought she might drink again, but she only swirled the wine around some more, staring into its depths. "Darla Pinkett was chosen for you. She was stepping out with Pete Clete, but he swore to the elders they hadn't, you know, 'done' anything. So Darla told them she'd been up in the barn loft with Jorah Ramsey. She hadn't, but Jorah was quick enough to back her up, so now they're getting married and she's no longer on the dinner list. Pete was furious, the idiot." Antonia laughed, hard and sharp. "He didn't know anything."

"Well, I do," snapped the dragon. "And there's an end of it." Flames! He wouldn't be sassed by an ignorant little chit of a human. She knew nothing.

But Antonia wasn't put off by his tone or the sparks shooting out between his teeth. "Prove it," she said, leaning forward. The firelight painted her face like a jack o' lantern's. "How do you 'know' I'm a maiden?"

"It's your . . . your . . ."

"What does being 'a maiden' even mean?"

The dragon suddenly, badly, wanted a gulp of her wine. "It means you're pure," he mumbled.

Antonia's grin increased an inch on either side. "Pure how? And why is pure desirable? If a cow craps, it makes a 'pure' cow pie, but it's not anything I'd want to put in my mouth."

"Look, dragons only consume maidens. Everyone knows that," said the dragon. Appeals to tradition often worked with villagers.

Not with Antonia. "Yes, but what is a maiden? Can you have kissed?"

"Yes, kisses are fine," said the dragon hurriedly. Antonia had a woman's shape; she'd probably kissed. She'd call foul if he nixed this one.

Resting her cheek in her palm, she turned over a ruby with the toe of her sturdy boot. Another jingle from beneath her layered hems. "How about . . . fondling?"

The dragon coughed. Antonia's chin jerked up. "You're embarrassed," she said.

"I am not." The dragon turned his head to study the scorch marks on the west wall.

"Your scales just turned a brighter shade of green," she said. He felt her scrutinizing him. "Now that I think about it, you're the only dragon anyone's seen in the valley. Does that mean you're a maiden?"

The dragon choked on his smoke. "See here, girl, I don't believe my personal affairs are any business of yours."

"Whereas you're allowed to know mine in detail?" she retorted.

They matched glares over the waning yellow firelight. "Be fair," she said after a moment. "Who am I going to tell your secrets anyway?"

There was that. And if she gave up her secrets, he'd know for certain if she was pure. He really didn't like his sudden doubt in his maiden-detecting skills.

He crossed his paws, drawing back his neck in an "S" curve. "You first," he said.

"I kissed Jack Wylie at the harvest festival," she said. "And Danny Bunn, although it was more a case of him kissing me."

"Is that all?" asked the dragon, running his tongue over his lips. Talking was hungry work, and under the faint odors of cow dung and hay, she smelled deliciously of blood, sweat, and girl.

She folded her arms, broken fingernails tapping against the goblet's gleaming side. "Your turn."

Grumbling, the dragon did his best to ignore the emptiness in his belly. "I flared my wings at a sow I met out flying one evening," he said.

"A sow?" Her eyes rounded. "You don't mean a female pig, surely."

"A lady dragon!" The dragon's shout echoed off the close, soot-smelling walls. "Sow's the proper term for them."

"No wonder they're reluctant to cozy up with you," muttered Antonia.

"I never said they were . . ." The dragon caught himself, seeing her smirk. "I believe it's your turn."

Her gaze went inward, dreamy, as she played with a stray golden-brown curl. "I went into the hay fields with Jack later that night."

The dragon's wings tensed. He wasn't too familiar with human mating customs, but he knew that if you put a male rabbit and a female rabbit alone together, certain activities often ensued. He'd heard young humans often behaved similarly. "And?" he prompted.

"And it's your turn again." She sipped her wine. "Flaring your wings at a sow doesn't sound particularly romantic."

"It's fairly significant."

He only heard the defensiveness in his voice when she

laughed. "Look." Dropping his gaze, he doodled with a claw on the cave floor. "Dragon reproduction is . . . complicated."

Antonia waited him out.

"There aren't a lot of us to begin with, and you've got to do your nest up properly before a sow will even look at you."

She held her goblet to the firelight. "So, that's the reason for all these sparklies."

"That's right. Now it's . . ."

"No." She shook her head. "All you've told me about is the wing-flaring. Is that all the contact you've had with a lady dragon?"

There's no one she can tell, he consoled himself. "Yes. What happened between you and this Jack?"

"Just a bit of cuddling," she said. She stared down into the goblet then drank the last of the wine with a toss of her head. "I got scared," she confessed, setting the goblet down with a little laugh. "Silly me. I should've been more scared of ending up on your menu, shouldn't I?"

The dragon laughed, too, relief tickling the fringe at the back of his neck. His instincts hadn't been wrong, then. "So you are a maiden, after all."

"Yes. As are you."

"Well, you don't usually apply human terminology to dragons."

"Of course not, of course not," she agreed. "But I don't think a bit of wing-flaring counts! After all, if waving at a boy took a girl off the maiden list, you'd starve." Her shoulders shook with merriment, skirts jingling. Her breath smelled of sweet wine. Her flesh would, too. The dragon inched forward, drooling.

"Yes, I suppose I would," he said.

Wiping her eyes with the back of one hand, Antonia reached down to rearrange her skirts. "A maiden dragon," she said and shook her head. "I suppose, if our positions were reversed, it would be entirely proper for me to eat you."

The dragon stopped, struck by the absurdity of the thought.

"I suppose it would be," he said and chuckled.

He was still laughing when Antonia whipped a crossbow from under her skirts and shot him accurately through the left eye.

Dragon steak proved excellent with hot sauce.

Early Birds

Paul Weidknecht

As she returned the phone to its cradle, Mildred patted her lips, gently tapping them with her fingertips, a nervous teenage gesture that had managed to stick around these sixty years later. She had disappointed herself once again. She was all prepared to say no, and she should have said no, but by the end of the conversation, yes had replaced it, making for yet another lunch appointment with Constance.

Then she brightened.

She could call Constance back, tell her the grandchildren were on their way over, that she had forgotten all about their visit. A moment later she looked down at the phone and shook her head. No, she thought, that won't work; grandmothers never forget grandchildren visits.

But any excuse would only postpone their lunch date. And the point *was* to cancel, to keep them canceled, and not to make any more.

Every other Tuesday, the two would go out to eat, always some place new, always before four. Sometimes they'd be running late and arrive at 3:51 or 3:53 or even 3:57 and the waitress—no, they're *servers* now—would slide two dinner menus in front of them prompting a scowl from Constance. At once, Constance would collect both menus and remind the person to bring the right ones. Mildred never caught the expression on the server's face because she'd be gazing out the window, embarrassed enough for all three of them.

For years, the orbits of their lives had intersected cordially, though not closely, but three weeks after Robert passed away, Constance phoned Mildred, her voice small and shaky, asking if she wanted to have lunch. Mildred agreed, thinking it would be nice to take some loneliness out of this woman's day, and perhaps it was her maudlin perception of their first dinner that caused the complaint by Constance ("This shrimp bisque is just not hot enough") to be viewed as a justifiable bother. After all, Mildred didn't like warm bisque, either, and asking for it hot was not unreasonable. However, after subsequent eating events gave rise to complaints about hardened rolls, limp salads, dirty silverware, lipstick-stamped glasses, a baked potato with a dark spot, and a steak served on a cold plate, it became clear that dining perfection was theoretical to Constance, something wished for but hopelessly unattainable.

Of course, the wait staff could never rectify the situation on their own. Several moments later, the manager would walk across the carpet in brisk step, looking over the tops of their heads until the last minute, smiling amiably with a slight bow once he was at the table. When the time came to concede a point in acquiescence, nearly every one of these managers would gesture in small harmless movements as if restrained in front by invisible handcuffs.

Then there was the matter of Constance and bread. A roll torn in half, the round portion secured between index finger and thumb, the ragged section blotting, sponging, mopping, then finally, painting the plate clean in five vertical stripes and a finishing horizontal wipe: dinner roll as squeegee. Mildred had tried staring at the plate, but Constance never looked up while she was painting and likely would have ignored the hint anyway. During these times, Mildred could think only of men with untamed facial hair sitting around campfires, tin plates on their laps, maybe a coyote howling in the background. Not long after, all uneaten rolls were napkin-clad and purse-bound, ending their dining experience for another fourteen days.

Mildred felt embarrassment should not figure so prominently in this dining arrangement. Embarrassment was for others, the young, the unaware, those stricken to bewilderment by the surprises of life's meandering ways. She was beyond that at her age, convinced that a quiet, dignified stoicism should mark these years of earned leisure.

But not every other Tuesday.

The Sea-Mist was new to them. Constance parked the car, and the two clopped up the wooden ramp every seafood restaurant seemed to possess. In the foyer sat an immaculate aquarium containing white gravel and unknown fish with fins trailing like silk streamers. Coarse nets and lobster pot markers hung on the walls, framing prints of oil paintings showing various maritime vessels; clippers, schooners, and other ships neither of them could identify. Polished brass portholes centered with mirrors decorated the wall between each booth where they now sat. Their server, a fit young woman with a pageboy and tattoo of a unicorn on her calf, appeared moments later.

Constance ordered the flounder stuffed with crabmeat and Mildred decided on the chicken parmigiana. Both were delighted to find the restaurant offered raspberry iced tea, and they ordered this minor indulgence as a break from their regular lemon wedge-and-sugar substitute faux-ade. After the server returned with the salads, Mildred found herself settling into the booth, pleased at this beginning. Not only had the server handed them the right menus—the early birds—where every entree was at least three dollars less than the regular dinner prices, she also had put the salad dressing in little plastic cups instead of pouring it over the salads. All in all, Mildred was quite optimistic about their early dinner.

"She's in a better place now," Constance began.

Mildred gasped. "Goodness, Gertrude died?"

"Oh no," Constance said, waving a hand, "She's at the Shady Birch Convalescent Center. I visited her yesterday, and she couldn't be happier. The rehab section has just been renovated. It's beautiful. Not like that last place."

Mildred wasn't sure *beautiful* was the right word for a rehabilitation center. She continued listening.

"Well, anyway, I hope it works out for her," Constance continued. "She should have said something to the administration of that last place. Some people let others walk all over them. Believe me, they would have known my feelings. You know me, if I don't like a meal, I tell them. I'm not going to sit in a restaurant, pay good money, and put up with a poor meal. People think they are being polite when they are really being weak."

Mildred decided to let it pass. Constance was in a good mood. After all, maybe she was talking about someone else.

Ten minutes later Mildred looked over at the swinging doors that led to the kitchen. Above the doors were two meals on a large serving tray supported by a palm bent backward. The tray hovered for a moment, then drifted forward as the swinging doors parted and snapped back with a squeak then a thump.

"I think these are ours," Mildred said.

Constance turned around in the booth. "Yum," she said, smiling.

The server lowered herself to one knee in front of the adjoining booth and slid the tray onto the table. One at a time, she picked up the plates with an oven mitten.

"These look wonderful," Constance said.

The server placed the meals in front of each woman. "Please be careful. The plates are very hot."

As soon as the server was gone, Constance leaned over her plate and inhaled deeply with her eyes were closed. Mildred mouthed a short prayer and grabbed a squat jar with a perforated metal lid, shaking grated cheese onto the mozzarella-covered cutlet and the spaghetti. Constance folded a lemon wedge, so the ends touched, dripping the juice over the flounder. For the first thirty seconds of the meal, they traded compliments about how appealing the other's meal looked. For the next five minutes, they ate wordlessly.

Mildred was convinced that while good food stimulated the sense of taste, there was always a higher function of the dining experience at work: the evocation of feeling. Presentation of food, the selection of elements and blending of ingredients in their right proportions, was art, true enough, yet the ultimate goal of fine eating was the creation of an emotion, that feeling of being together with family and friends from a time past. She understood how a song or poem or film could be used as a vehicle for emotion, for something deep and contemplative, and now realized the same could be said for food. Without a doubt, the human body had to contain a nerve—more like a bundle of them—connecting the taste buds to the heartstrings.

A half hour later, Mildred stopped eating. Her meal was unfinished. Constance looked up from her plate.

"What's the matter?"

Mildred said nothing as she turned her plate toward her friend. Constance's face went slack.

"We have to talk to the manager about this," Constance said. "We need to get the manager. What's our girl's name?"

"Nora. I think."

Mildred heard the swinging doors open, then close, and saw the manger walking toward them. He was staring directly at her. Mildred caught something in his face, a look of determination, maybe annoyance. He was not smiling.

Now she wished she had said nothing. She wanted to take the complaint back, start anew, walk up the wooden ramp again, and order something different.

"Hello, ma'am, my name is Sal. I'm the manager. How may I help you?" Sal's hands were not folded in front of him. Mildred felt a sudden heat come onto her neck and ears.

"Yes, why hello, yes," Mildred stammered. "I was eating my meal and, well, I'm almost finished and I find this sitting on the bottom of the plate." She angled the plate toward him like a jeweler showing an expensive watch, but without the smile.

The manager leaned in for a better view, dipping to avoid the plate's glare. His eyes widened for a moment, then narrowed.

The long black hairs sat pasted in place by the reddish-orange sauce.

Not one hair, several. Certainly, too many to have been an accidental thread breaking free from a scalp and floating plate-ward. It was all very clear to Mildred. She could imagine the kitchen staff, tattooed and unshaven, smoking at a half-opened back door, laughing about it right now, the only break in their mirth occurring when the conversation turned to which one of them had the most stringent parole conditions.

The manager cleared his throat. "I'm sorry, ma'am. I'll speak to the kitchen staff about this. I appreciate your bringing this to my attention."

Constance and Mildred looked at each other. Constance turned toward the manager.

"Well, what are you going to do about it?"

"As I said, ma'am, I will speak to the staff and correct the situation."

"That's it?"

The manager continued. "Ma'am, that is all I can do right now."

"Correcting the situation," Mildred said, "would be comping us the meal."

Immediately, Mildred regretted that word, *comping*. It wasn't feminine or dignified or stoic. It sounded crass, slick, like something a parolee would say. Or Constance.

"Ladies, please, I'm trying to make this right," Sal said.

"Talking to your staff isn't helping us," Mildred said. "And it *isn't* making it right."

This surge of assertion exhilarated Mildred. These words coming from her mouth were strange and exciting. And that look on Sal's face.

But what surpassed even this was the look on Constance's face. The woman's eyes were full of light as if a piece of sunlight had gotten caught behind each iris. Mildred was sure it was the angle of the sun. Had to be the sun. But as she studied her closely, Mildred realized something else. Constance was more than happy. She was proud.

"Ma'am, you have eaten nearly all of that meal. I won't be able to adjust your check. I'm sorry. I'll have Nora total it out. She'll be here shortly." Sal turned and walked toward the kitchen.

Constance and Mildred looked to each other. The piece of sunlight? Gone. Mildred looked toward the swinging doors and saw Sal giving Nora instructions.

"Why, what a rude man," Constance said.

⌇

"Like I said," Constance explained as she drove. "I cannot, cannot, believe that man. We should've never been charged for that meal. That was disgusting. 'I'll have Nora total it out.' We weren't even offered dessert. And dessert comes with the early bird. That's fraud! We should find out who owns that Sea . . . Shell . . . whatever it's called."

"Mist," Mildred said quietly.

"He was very rude to us. You can tell he's not a professional. This is probably his first job managing a restaurant."

"No," Mildred replied. "It's not."
Constance frowned in confusion. "What do you mean? Why that was the first time we'd been to that Sea-Spray place."

"Sea-Mist. Yes, it was. But that wasn't the first time we've seen that manager."

"What are you talking about, Mildred?"

"He was the manager of The Trawler. He must have changed restaurants. He recognized us."

"The Trawler?"

Mildred nodded. "Yes. Over on the bay."

"Did that place have a wooden ramp going up to the door?" Constance asked.

"I'm sure of it."

Constance's face changed slowly, and she nodded. "Oh, that's right. The Trawler. Sure. We got half off the check because I started to get sick. I think it was the fried clam strips. Too chewy."

Mildred and Constance looked at each other and began to laugh, knowing the Tuesday after next was only fourteen days away.

Breakfast for One

GEOFFREY MEHL

Frank settled into the familiar third booth of the Puffin Diner and glanced at the passing traffic outside. He savored the unusually quiet room: soft conversations at the counter, the light clatter of flatware against sturdy china, the murmured dialogue that tumbled from the kitchen.

Within moments, Martha approached in a crisp waitress uniform. She produced an order pad and gentle smile, brushed a strand of hair away from her cheek and said, "Good to have you back, Frank." She lifted a pen and asked, "The usual?"

Frank was about to nod, then astonished himself with a pause. His eyes roamed the table, the tidy array of condiments and the sanctuary of menus in vinyl folders and finally the vacant space opposite him.

He took a breath. "Well, maybe not."

Her smile evaporated, and her eyebrow jumped upward.

He sensed confusion but ignored Martha's reaction and escaped into the open menu before him.

Martha's pen hovered over the pad. "So, uh, not the usual?"

The usual, Frank thought. Every day, for years, longer than Martha had been the waitress. Granola with skim milk. Egg substitute, scrambled, no salt. Whole wheat toast, no butter, no jam. Small glass of cranberry juice, decaf coffee. All as routine as his entire life.

"You're sure about this?" Martha asked with her pen poised.

Frank continued to study the menu and found the nerve to raise his hand and gesture for a moment to consider alternatives.

Impatience crept into her voice. "Do you need another minute or so?"

Frank drew another breath, deeper this time. "No. Let's see. I'd like two, no, make it three eggs, regular eggs, up. Plus some pancakes, maybe three or four. And some sausage, with home fries."

"The Number Three platter? That's got two eggs, any way you like, with a short stack of pancakes and two sausages. Or bacon if you prefer. Cheaper than ordering separately."

Frank furrowed his brow and continued to stare at the menu. "Hm. No, I'd like three eggs. And extra sausages would be good. Plus a big glass of orange juice. And coffee."

"Decaf?"

"Regular. And instead of toast, an English muffin, with butter. No, wait. A Danish, the one with the cherry or strawberry."

"You're kidding, right?"

Frank looked up and gave her a faint but firm smile. "No. Not at all."

Martha studied the order pad.

"Okay, three eggs up, pancakes, extra sausages, OJ, regular coffee, cherry Danish."

He folded his hands on the menu. "Don't forget the home fries."

"You're really, really sure about this, Frank?"

Frank responded with a serene smile.

Martha sighed, wrote the addition, then offered an expression of sympathy. "Oh, and we were all very sorry to hear about your loss. Our condolences."

Frank nodded then brightened. "I wonder: could I get an order of bacon on the side?"

Bump and Run

Diane Sismour

After riding public transportation to work for three years, I've learned not to gasp, make comments, or laugh, while eavesdropping on all the juicy gossip of lives more interesting than my own. The bus is crammed with passengers, and I'm having trouble picking just one topic to listen to with so many conversations going on around me. At least until the two women sitting behind me ply the question women have speculated upon since the beginning of time.

"I've met men in bars, I tried dating services, where can I meet a nice guy?" asks one of the women.

This pings my radar. I'm expecting to hear the bowling alley, the library, speed dating, the beach—my list could fill a diary.

"You're never going to believe it. My roommate met her man at the grocery store," says the second woman.

Completely forgetting the aforementioned self-imposed rules, I snort a laugh and blurt out, "The grocery store . . . in which aisle, pet foods or home supplies?"

The conversation behind me stops. Our entire area goes dead silent, too. I guess there are a lot of us looking for love in the wrong places.

The friend asks, "How do you meet someone in the grocery store?"

"Friday night is singles night. If you like what's in someone's cart, you bump buggies to start a conversation."

Weird, but simple, I think, instead of blurting out my inner snark. I've gone to worse meet-and-greets. One was at a funeral home. The entire night screamed desperation.

The thought of grocery shopping for a man perplexed me all day long. Where to begin? Do I search the home goods aisle for a handyman or the pets aisle near the dog food? A man with a dog sounds attractive, kind of a two for one deal. Men with cats make me think of Doctor Evil, not an ideal image for a guy in my eyes. Then there's the frozen pizzas and ice cream section. At least I'll know how to cook the food.

My casual Friday clothes aren't date-wear, but if I add more makeup, the outfit will do just fine. In any other part of the country, I might be considered pretty, but in South Beach, where exotic is normal, my looks are subpar. I have to win a date with my charming personality. *Geesh, now I'm giving myself eye rolls.*

I remove the pins that hold my long, brunette hair into the usual, respectable bun, and finger comb to loosen the knot. Then apply a brush of bronzer here, a smear of lip gloss there, and perfect . . . or good enough for grocery shopping. Instead of disembarking at the usual stop, I continue several more blocks past the Boulevard to the supermarket.

The store must be crowded because there are barely any shopping carts available. Beside a vending machine, stands a lone buggy. After rolling a few feet, I know why this one remains. A front wheel doesn't turn properly. The entire store is quiet compared to the racket emanating from the stubborn wheel.

I thump and squeak through the store to the frozen foods. Occasionally, there are men contemplating between pepperoni and plain, but finding one who even appeals to me is rarer than a perfectly cooked steak. From Haagen-Dazs ice cream pints to frozen waffles, there is nobody in this section.

"Where is everyone?"

A somewhat attractive man rolls my way. He's not much taller than I am; his body appears toned beneath his T-shirt, with a next-day beard shadowing his jaw.

He looks me up and down, then appraises my empty cart. His contains three meat-lovers, thick-crust pies.

"Yum." Before I can knock buggies to start a conversation, he backs away and high-tails it out of frozen foods. My crooked wheel amplifies in the nearly vacant aisle as I hurry after him. When I turn the corner, he's gone. He left the cart behind. I can see him rounding the turn at the end of the next aisle.

You can't escape me that easily. I stalk him all the way to the fruits and vegetable department.

"So here is where the crowd is congregating," I say to no one in particular.

I lurk from a distance. Men are casually perusing the aisle in search of companionship. Women are primping, twirling their hair, and doing their best to inspect the fruit in a provoca-tive manner by fondling the zucchini and cucumbers to lure a desired match. *Note to self: if purchasing fresh produce, buy it earlier in the week.* The heavy-handed application of flowery perfumes, musky colognes, and the aroma of overly handled fruit, mingles into an ill-concocted fruit salad for the olfactory.

Instead of Jane Simmons, I pretend that I'm Dr. Jane Goodall watching the mating rituals of Homo sapiens. A male circles behind a female, who is interacting with another male. He selects a large melon. I'll call the intruder brown-eyes and the challenged male, blue-eyes. Brown-eyes strokes the melon and engages in conversation with her. Blue-eyes maneuvers his cart between the female and brown-eyes, and then stands taller, blocking further interaction with the female. The rejected male moves on to another female, while the winning blue-eyes puffs his chest. At least he didn't thump it with his fists.

A whiff of sandalwood invades my area before a cart bumps

into mine. Stunned at the intrusion into my personal space I blurt, "What the hell is wrong with you?" Then, remembering the Friday night dating game, in a far more pleasant tone I say, "Oh, hi. So what brings you here?"

At first, the six-foot-fourish metro-sexual Adonis appears stunned, but a megawatt smile brightens the entire citrus section before he says, "Grocery shopping? You just ran into my cart."

"I did?" I'm pretty certain my cart hadn't moved. At once, I rethink the situation. Who am I to complain? The man is too gorgeous, and totally not someone who would ever give me a second glance, but what the heck . . . when in Rome.

He looks into my still empty cart. "Not much of a cook, are you," he says, more as a statement than a question.

"That obvious, huh? I can't help it if my cooking abilities have an unimaginative palate."

"First time cart-banging?" he asks.

"You could say that." Instead of giving him a huge eye roll that the question deserved, I think of a way to change the subject. His buggy contains some unusual tropical fruits, a jumbo bar of dark chocolate, and the largest cucumber I've ever seen. "And who are you trying to pick up here, a porn star? Aren't you overcompensating just a little?" My hands measure six inches apart, then eight inches. I stop moving them at ten.

His smile deepens with each motion into a mischievous grin. "Why, whatever do you mean?" he says, in guilty innocence.

"You deserve this." I give him a huge eye roll.

Laugh lines crinkle around his eyes, and dimples pinch his perfectly sculpted cheeks as he laughs. "Would you like a cup of coffee?"

"Only if you can explain this Friday night bump thing to me." Who am I kidding? If he were a lemming, I'd follow him off a cliff.

"Deal. My feet are killing me. I had four bridal parties with updos today without a break." He removes his man-purse off his shoulder and places the messenger-styled leather bag into the cart before leading the way to the café.

Leave it to me to run into someone not interested in women. However, he did run into my cart. And, he didn't run away after I snapped at him for ramming me. Maybe I can just relax and be myself—the non-flirty, not watch-my-every-word, me. A girl can always hope.

I thump, and he rolls, to the coffee nook toward the front of the store. No one approaches me, bumps my cart, or cares that I'm not in the least interested in playing their game. However, he is prime pickings to the other shoppers.

The Adonis zigs and zags around the approaching primates with ease. "The soon-to-be bride wanted this elaborate braided style on a ponytail budget. She was sweet with big brown doe-eyes. I couldn't turn her down. It took hours to create the sea-shell beehive she wanted, and so worth every aching knuckle."

Two of my strides equal one of his, and I'm doing my best to stay behind him. So are half the women and a few of the men he is passing. I restrain from turning all roller-derby-queen on them, after reconsidering the possibility of so much blood and mayhem over a cup of java with a god. I nudge the closest pursuer into a cardboard display, sending cupcake decorations rolling across the floor.

"Oops." So much for my restraint. The rest back off in search of easier prey. Alone, we stop at the barista's counter.

He steps to the register, and the cashier's eyes widen as he towers before her. When he smiles, she moves her hand uncon-sciously to her heart. "A skinny grande latte." He steps aside for me to order, breaking the trance.

"A small coffee with medium sugar, medium cream, please."

cExasperated, I change the order, "On second thought, can you just add skimmed milk?"

A satisfied smile graces his lips. "And two double-chunk chocolate cookies. I've got this," he says, waving me off as he pays the bill.

Now he's talking my language—chocolate. Within minutes, we are sitting across from each other in the café area eager to share sinful cookies. I'm ready to hear the dirt on the Friday night dating scene.

He extends a large hand. "I'm Adrian, owner of Celestial Salon and Day Spa."

"Jane Simmons, receptionist to the want-to-be stars at Felix's Model and Talent Agency."

His hand dwarfs mine as we exchange pleasantries. I notice that my fingertips are in dire need of a manicure compared to his neat and clear-polished nails.

The rough cuticles don't escape his attention either. He captures my fingers with his. "You should make an appointment with me tomorrow. Someone with such lovely hair should have nails to match."

His thumb skims along my fingertips before releasing mine. Zings jolt up each finger. Snatching my ratty cuticles away, I smooth my pencil skirt to hide both hands beneath the table. I realize he's waiting for an answer.

My brain is still contemplating the why behind the zing, and it takes a moment before I remember what's on the schedule. Of all days for me to have to chaperone models on a shoot.

"No can do; I'm booked solid tomorrow. I'll take a raincheck, though," I say.

He sits straighter, giving himself more time to recover from my rejection. Disappointment clouds his face, for the briefest moment, before recovering his charm. Adrian removes a silver case from his man purse and hands me a business card.

Our fingers touch again as I reach for the card, and more static jolts my hand. This time, I'm not the only one affected because the ivory linen stock with simple, bold print drops between us onto the table. He retrieves it and with a curious expression, slides both his business card and the small white plate laden with a giant cookie in front of me.

Retrieving his information, I place the card beside my plate and watch as he breaks his baked good into quarters. He dips one into the latte before devouring the huge bite. A look of utter joy beams from his face. He waits before dipping the next section to watch as I bite into my confection.

The cookie is crunchy on the outside and soft on the inside. My eyes close in enjoyment as the rick dark chocolate drizzled over the chunky chip wafts in layers of yumfest. "Thank you," I say after the taste orgasm subsides.

"Trust me. Watching you eat was my pleasure. So, you know something about me, but I don't know anything about you yet. What brought you here tonight?"

"I heard about this meet and greet while on the bus, and wanted to see if the hype was true. From the looks of it, the vegetable aisle is the new meat market."

He nods in agreement before savoring his last bite. I watch Adrian smooth a lock of golden hair away from his cheek to behind his ear. His skin is flawless. He spends much more time pampering than I do. He deserves a goddess beside him, someone with impeccable style and not a hair out of place. He is not here looking for me.

Then I think of the electric snap when his fingers held mine and begin fantasizing how my body would react if his hands slid over more than my knuckles. My mouth goes dry, and I can feel my eyes about to glaze over. Before my mind completely evaporates, I ask, "So, how does this meet-up work?"

"Women shop for themselves and rely on their appearance to connect with a match, but men select items they think will attract someone to them."

"Interesting. So I just look for the cart that best describes me."

"In a matter of speaking. What are you looking for?" His cheeks flush, "Obviously not a giant cucumber."

"There is nothing wrong with an oversized cucumber. So long as it's prepared properly," I say. My eyes widen at the verbal faux pas.

His eyes glint in intrigue. "Properly?" he asks with far more curiosity than a cucumber deserves.

The game begins. I glance down at my hands fidgeting on my lap and slide them under my thighs to still them. I'm so out of practice at sparring innuendoes, and my cooking skills are why I head straight to the already prepared and seasoned departments. Think, Jane. How is a cucumber prepared?

"You know, stripped, and seeded," I say, finally.

By the heat flooding my face, I'm definitely not wearing enough bronzer to conceal the blush crawling to my hairline. The thought of how my brain just scrambled that plain speak into sexy verbiage spikes the heat into my scalp.

His smile broadens. His eyes darken to a deep Caribbean blue. "You still haven't answered the question."

My mind is replaying the conversation, but I'm stuck on the way his face perked up when he asked, properly. "Do you mean, what am I searching for?"

His attention focuses on my sweep of hair as far as the table would allow, and slowly returns up to my eyes. "Sweetheart, do you take me as a man who is looking for a one-sided relationship?"

Did I hear him right? He just said relationship. At first I'm stunned, and sip the coffee to stall to formulate a coherent answer. "I think if someone learned enough about me to cook a perfect steak, then we must be compatible."

He pops the last bite into his mouth. I'm staring as he chews. His upper lip is thinner, with a full bottom lip I'd like to bite. When his coffee cup blocks the view, I snap to the present.

Adrian is smiling, and concentrating entirely on me. His gaze penetrates my defenses. "And how do you prefer your meat?"

Is he referring to steak or, um, cucumbers? Maybe he is looking for someone like me, especially after that relationship comment. I might not know how to grill, but I'm pretty good with a menu. He's still expecting an answer. "Medium rare?"

His eyes glint with awareness of my discomfort. "The most particular to cook. A good grilling challenge."

His cell rings, interrupting our moment. "Yes, Miguel. Okay, I'll be right there." He pockets the phone. "I apologize, but Miss Florida insists on fresh highlights before leaving for Atlantic City."

Darn, just when things were getting interesting.

He slides his chair back, stands before me, and extends his hand to take mine. He gives me a lopsided smile, "You have my number. Call whenever you'd like that manicure . . . or steak." He bends to kiss my fingertips.

Tingles race up my arm, down my body, and come to a slow happy boil low in my stomach. I close my eyes for a moment and pray that he's not playing games with my affections. When they open, he is gone. "So like a god. A flash here, zing there, and poof, he disappears."

Straightening his card before me, I search blindly in my purse and pull out the cell. I press the numbers to dial, "Let's see if he's telling me the truth."

The phone rings only once before a cultured Hispanic voice answers, "Celestial Salon. Miguel at your service. How may I help you today?"

"Hi. I'd like an appointment for a manicure with Adrian on Sunday."

"I'm sorry Madam. He doesn't take appointments on Sundays."

Disappointed, I say, "I'd still like to make an appointment." Miguel gives me an available time, and I schedule the information into my phone's calendar.

After disconnecting, I walk to where we left our groceries at the café's entrance and take his cart instead of mine to the register line. His selections are far more interesting than I would have picked. There is one way to find out what I'm buying. After pressing the code tagged on each one, the self-checkout blurts in an electronic voice, one Toblerone, one kumquat, one passion fruit, one English cucumber.

I hold the enormous vegetable nimbly in my hand, before placing the phallus into the plastic bag.

A woman waiting behind me says, "That's a nice cucumber. Are you making gazpacho?"

"Something like that."

~

The next morning, the sun bursts through the only window with a partial view of the ocean in my one-room loft. A strip of light warms my face awakening me from the image of Adrian's sparkling-white, celebrity smile biting into a large cucumber.

A psychologist would have a field day interpreting that dream. It has me wondering what my subconscious is conjuring. My physical reaction, after dreaming about his hands working the kinks out of my lower back, is not as subtle. The same glow I felt when he focused all his attention on me after I had taken the first bite of cookie is radiating through my body.

My job is far less glamorous than the title, Model Consultant Associate, sounds. I'm just a glorified babysitter to make sure the talent and the contractors arrive for the shoots. I try taking the time to look better for work today, but my hair isn't cooperating, and I end up twisting it into the usual knot and pinning the bulk into place. Trying to stand out among models is useless anyway.

The site is on the Hilton Bentley rooftop overlooking South Beach. The calendar might read September, but next year's beachwear is today's shoot. Makeup brushes flutter over the bodies of one male and two female models to conceal skin tone flaws. The lighting is set up and ready for camera checks. The photographer is almost ready. *Where the heck is the hair stylist?* Thirty minutes pass and I make an executive decision before the other contractors start leaving.

Adrian's card is in my hand, and I'm calling his salon. "Please let him be available."

"Celestial Salon, Adrian at your service. How may I help you today?" His voice alone sends tendrils of zings skittering along my skin.

"Hi, Adrian. We met last night at the supermarket."

"Are you ready for a manicure, Jane, or should I fire up the grill?"

I can hear the heat in his voice and my heart races. His invitation meant far more than sharing a good meal. It's been a long time since I shared more than a good meal. Phew, for a second my mind goes blank. All I want to say is yes to his question. A comb skitters across the concrete rooftop to my feet reminding me of my mission.

"I need you—I need your help. It's a styling emergency. I'm on the Bentley's roof with three models and no hair personnel. The photographer is ready to walk."

"I'll be there in ten minutes. And Jane, thank you." His call ends.

As if on cue, Adrian walks through the doorway, to an empty table set up beside wardrobe, and prepares his station. Without a glance in my direction, he opens a soft-sided briefcase brimming with styling tools and product. In moments, he has the male model camera-ready with a few sweeps of hair gel finger-brushed through his shoulder-length, seemingly sunkissed hair.

With his attention focused on the first woman, I watch him twist her chin-length, bright-red hair into a loose braided crown. Tendrils frame her cheeks, and wisps soften the nape, perfect for the gold metallic tunic she's wearing. Model two joins the first on the staging set.

The second woman has long, thick, wavy hair similar to mine. I'm interested to see how he transforms me—I mean her—into a picture-ready goddess. His first attempt, to apply only macadamia oil, leaves too many flyaway strands. I could have told him that.

Adrian looks at me. His attentive look softens when he smiles. He twirls his finger motioning me to spin.

The bikini-clad model strolls past me moments later with a sloppy knot hanging just above her left shoulder. Her easy styling makes me realize how little I did to prepare for work today. She is pulling off the relaxed elegance far better than I do.

Is that how he sees me? A sloppy knot . . . really? I find the compact mirror in my purse and do a quick hair exam. Half the bobby pins are falling out, and his creation looks very similar to my mess, barely hanging together. So long as he likes it, I guess it's fine.

The flash is blinding as Stephan takes shots from multiple camera angles at a rapid fire. At the very least, I expect Adrian to stand beside me before he has to redo hair. Instead, he's walking along and chatting with the photographer, not even making eye contact with me.

There are several wardrobe changes and hair touch-ups before the afternoon light moves to early evening. Stephan finally turns away and flips his wrist to dismiss the session. The models leave the staged area to prepare for the next set beside the pool bar. Adrian hurries to his station and changes their appearances toward sleek resort evening looks after they switch wardrobes.

The male talent's styling isn't much different. The second model's red hair now has a low side-part slicked smooth behind her ears. The last model's change is dramatic. Her hair is stunning in a loose side-swept fishbone-braid that lies across her collarbone.

This time Adrian stands beside me as the photographer races to catch the perfect shots before the sun sets.

"You inspire me. I can't wait to play with your hair."

The blissful thoughts of him playing with any part of me instantly evaporated my irritation from the cold shoulder he gave me earlier. "You presume a lot," I say, teasing.

The crew continues working, but my attention drifts from the shoot to the spectacular view overlooking the ocean. Everyone else become indiscernible as I watch the sky meld into hues of oranges, pinks, and purples. I can still hear the waves crashing along the shore above the traffic noise.

Adrian stands behind me, blocking the early evening breeze as the sun dips below the horizon. "Thank you for calling me today."

"Are you kidding? You saved my butt."

His hands rub warmth into my arms, then kneads the knots from the top of my shoulders, working towards my neck. He pulls the remaining pins, freeing my hair. His fingers caress my neck, releasing the day's tension, as only a hairdresser knows how.

"Are we done for today? We could go back to my place and grill a couple steaks," he says.

Between his hands kneading me into jelly, and his invitation turning my fortitude to goo, all I want to do is melt all over him like glaze on a donut. As much as I'd love to take Adrian up on his offer, spending time alone with him at his house feels too soon in our fledgling relationship. "You're done, but I have to head back to the office. I'll take a rain check, though."

Stephan joins us. "Great talent today, Jane. Is the beach shoot still on for Wednesday?"

This week is crammed full with appointments and remembering them all is impossible. I check my cell phone's calendar and then check the weather. "Yes. We're meeting at 6:00 a.m. in the lobby."

Adrian reaches for my cell and checks my schedule. "Don't you take any time off?"

"Not when there's catalog shoots. September is the agency's busiest month," I say.

"Good job with hair today, dude," says Stephan. "I have a couple gigs coming up. Do you want to grab a beer, and I can fill you in?"

Adrian looks from Stephan to me. "Do you want to join us? Oh, right, you have work to finish," he says.

"You guys go ahead," I say, mentally kicking myself. Using Stephan as a buffer would have been the perfect opportunity to get to know Adrian better. Sigh. I'll be microwaving another frozen dinner tonight. My stomach growls as I think how much better a grilled steak would taste, with him for dessert.

Sunday morning I wake to another dream. This time Adrian is brushing chocolate onto my fingernails. His blue eyes are intent on mine. Just before the dream fades, he sucks the chocolate off my index finger and says, "You are delectable."

I don't need a shrink to decipher this dream for me. Today is my manicure appointment at Celestial Salon and Day Spa. Maybe I should also pamper myself with a pedicure, just in case he enjoys pretty toes, too.

I'm ready to jump out of bed and search the kitchen cabinets for anything with cocoa but know better than to look. Last night I ate the Swiss chocolate while watching *Entertainment Tonight.* They were featuring the Miss America contestants. I have to say, Miss Florida's highlights looked natural. Adrian did an amazing job coloring her hair.

I arrive for my appointment fifteen minutes early. The front desk is faux Greek columns with a black marble countertop. The flooring is large marble tiles in a swirl of storm cloud grays, with light blue walls. Local art hangs for sale around the entry. The hair stations are to the left, manicure tables are on the right, and the pedicure chairs and other service rooms are out of view. It's a masculine guise for a salon, even if the god brought touches of Athens with him.

Miguel is standing behind the counter. "Please choose your color and wait in the quiet room," He hands me a services menu and he points to an array of shallow shelves with nail polish in every color imaginable lining the wall behind me. OPI makes a color called "Milk Chocolate." I can't resist selecting it, especially after this morning's dream.

The quiet room has ocean sounds piped in, with seats sectioned off by softly lit screens. I peruse the list of options. Two types of facials catch my eye. One uses passion fruit, and the other uses kumquat as natural exfoliates. That explains the exotic fruit in Adrian's cart. However, I don't see anything using cucumbers. Oh hell, I have to try the passion fruit facial, too.

When the nail technician escorts me to her station, I relay my request to Miguel. He remains very calm. Instead of panicking at the ninety-minutes of additional services, he shifts the schedule on a touch screen that appears busier than my calendar. A gleaming smile preludes his answer.

"Yes, Miss Jane. We can accommodate your request."

"I wish my entire life could transform as easily at the touch of a screen," I say more to myself than him.

"Then life would become too easy," he says. "But transformations are what we do best, so relax, and enjoy."

A girl can get spoiled in here.

The woman leading me to her station detours to the pedicure area. "Miss Jane, I'm Teresa. We'll start with your pedicure first. After your polish dries, Marie will take over for the facial. Then you're with me again for the manicure."

A pedicure is far more than just someone painting your toes. The technician gives me a calf and foot therapy with hot stones, followed by rubbing essential oils into the skin to re-moisturize after so much exfoliation. The chocolate-colored polish is just the icing on the toes.

Teresa returns me to the quiet room. Small trays of cucumber sandwiches with scalloped edges and a tall pitcher of ice water with cucumber slices wait on the side table. Now the need for the large seedless cucumber in Adrian's cart makes so much more sense. "And here I thought he was just measuring up! Color me embarrassed," I say to myself.

"That was one of last year's polishes: a deep blush," says a familiar voice coming from behind me. I turn towards him, careful not to mess the polish.

Adrian stands in the doorway in a dark polo shirt, worn jeans, with a one-sided grin. Before I can say anything, he sits in the chair beside me, pours a glass of water, and then removes two tiny sandwiches from the tray onto a napkin, and places them in front of me. "Are you enjoying yourself?"

"I have very happy feet," I say, wiggling my toes in the one-size-fits-all foam sandals. They look like snorkel flippers on my size-six feet.

Before he can comment, Marie walks in to collect me for the next service.

"So, I'll see you later?" I ask.

"Absolutely. Who do you think is painting your nails?"

"Oh," is all I can manage to say before this morning's dream slams forward in my mind. My mouth goes dry in anticipation, and I down the water before we get past the manicure tables.

Marie makes quick work of preparing me for the facial. I'm relaxed from the pedicure, and the ocean sounds coming through the speakers make me forget that I'm in a building. By the time she exfoliates, extracts, soothes, smoothes, and moisturizes, I am ready for a nap.

"Come out when you're ready," she says, before disappearing out the door.

I relax for several minutes and luxuriate in anticipation of who is giving me my next service. My silky tank top slides over my freshly moisturized shoulders, and the skirt glides over my calves. I strap my sandals on instead of walking into the hallway with the foam fins.

Maria delivers me to the manicure station, I'm expecting to see Adrian, but instead, Teresa is gathering supplies for the next treatment. To say I wasn't looking forward to him playing out my delusion is a lie. It was a silly dream. One he didn't know about, or I hope he would have stuck around.

She places two bowls filled with clear glass beads and a liquid with a lavender aroma before me. After removing what's left of my current polish, she places each hand in the silky smooth liquid. The beads clink the glass as I absentmindedly trace my fingers through them.

I wonder why he left. The disappointment coursing through me is a surprise. Unfortunately, my subconscious has worked a lot of overtime. I hardly know the man. Apparently, gods are just like all the rest of the men I've met . . . too good to be true.

I'm sure she did a good job refining my fingertips. They look fabulous, but after expecting Adrian to relive my dream, a manicure is just a manicure.

Teresa relays me to the front desk and Miguel steps back. His ready smile beaming, "You look radiant, Miss Jane. Did you enjoy the afternoon?"

"Yes, thank you. Everyone is so nice, and I feel so relaxed."

Before I can remove my wallet, Miguel says, "There is no need. Your serves are already paid."

"Thank you. Adrian?"

He nods and answers the ringing phone.

I mouth the words, "Please tell him thank you for me."

He holds up a finger to stop me from leaving. "Can you please hold one minute, Madame," he says into the phone and hands me a small white envelope. "Adrian left this note for you."

"Thank you, Miguel." My first thought is to tear it open, but I refrain. At least until I reach the car. Fresh manicure be damned, I'm using my fingernail as a letter opener and prying the white card through the slit.

Jane, it reads, *I would like to see you again soon. From looking at your calendar, I know you are very busy this week, but hope you can meet on Friday night where we first met. We have to select our steaks. Adrian.*

He would like to see me? Does he mean in the citrus department or the café? And no salutations? All I ever hear is that women are hard to understand. Men are a confusing species all their own. Jane Goodall should have studied them instead of apes. I need better resources to snag a god.

The added salon service leaves little time to do all the regular chores I have lined up for this afternoon. My house can stay dirty until next weekend. Laundry and going for a run top the list. I have to work off some calories if I expect to eat any more cookies with Adrian. But I feel so relaxed and calm, a nap would be better than laundry, or running, or most things. No, not most things, having clean clothes to wear is better than dreaming about the impossible.

My definition for a Monday: if something can go wrong, it's bound to happen. Tuesday morning isn't much better, but I manage to double check with the contractors and talent for Wednesday's photo shoot. The stylist scheduled arrives, and Adrian's services aren't necessary. *Disappointing.*

Wednesday's catalog shoot turns into Thursday selecting

proofs to deliver on Friday. My schedule pushes later as more interruptions compound the day. I'm working, wondering where the week went, and how to dress for my date in the café, or grocery shopping if he doesn't show. Everyone is leaving the office at five p.m., and there's still a huge pile of work to finish. I call Adrian's salon number, and it goes directly to messages.

It's after six, and I still haven't heard back from him. Although it's not his fault my schedule is so crazy busy. After knocking my head against the desk, I close my laptop. I have a date with a god.

People are shoulder to shoulder in the produce aisle. I forgo the cart, weave from the fresh greens, to melons, and end my search for Adrian near citrus. He isn't here. He didn't wait for me.

If the despair is equivalent to the anticipation of seeing him again, the emptiness I'm feeling is bottomless. This calls for a pint of Haagen-Dazs. Maybe two.

I trudge through the empty aisles and turn towards frozen foods. Adrian is leaning against the cooler between pepperoni and plain, and in his cart are more varieties of steak than I knew existed. The smile that beams when he notices me evaporates the gloom in my heart.

"So, are you ready for that steak?" he asks.

There's so much more to his question. Are you hungry? Are you ready for a relationship? Your place or mine?

"Yes." To everything.

Hard Times

Jerry McFadden

"Are we going to eat him or not?"

"You think he's dead yet?"

The three of us looked over at the body partly hidden in the dark at the far edge of the camp. We had been thinking about it, but no one wanted to be the first to bring it up. Chan had stopped moaning about two hours ago. Jameson finally walked over to kick him in the leg to see if he would react. He didn't.

"It doesn't seem right to eat the cook."

True enough. Chan was, or had been, our cook and a damn good one at that. He came up with some weird ideas, such as fried grasshoppers, or wild onions, or cactus pears, or other weird tidbits that he found in odd places, but he also knew how to cook a fine dinner of beef or venison or rabbits or small birds, all with beans and biscuits.

"I never ate Chinese before," Rogers said.

"I have," I replied. "In 'Frisco. But they had noodles and all kinds of spices. Rice, too. Wasn't bad."

"We ain't got no noodles," Jameson said.

Rogers nodded. "I bet Chan could have come up with some spices, if he was the one still alive and thinking of eating one of us."

We looked at him again. We had extracted all of the arrows out of poor old Chan but had probably caused as much damage pulling them out as they had done going in. But one or two of them had probably hit a vital spot on the way in, so it wasn't our fault he died. But it surely added to our woes. We were lost and on foot in the desert, not having eaten for three days. A raggedy-ass band of Indians stole our horses in the night while we were sleeping. Chan got up to pee at the wrong moment, and they shot him full of those damn arrows.

"Died with his hand on his pecker," Rogers said.

"Every man's dream," Jameson noted.

"I ain't gonna eat his pecker."

"Didn't get any arrows in it."

"Don't care. Still ain't gonna eat it."

The Indians weren't coming back. They knew we were going to die out here, one way or the other. They would circle back to check on us now and them, to collect our guns, and maybe our clothes, without a fight.

"We could eat ol' Henry instead," Rogers said.

We all surveyed the mule. Just skin and bones. His ribs stuck out like wooden slats around a barrel. He shuffled around in the dark, bleating in protest against his hobbles. The Indians hadn't bothered to steal him. Even starving Indians have standards.

"Old Henry can still carry things, you know." Jameson pointed out. "We still have Chan's pot and pans and our bed rolls, saddles, and rifles. No point in carrying all of that. Old Henry can carry it all, plus the water, as far as he can. Then we eat him when he dies."

It was a plan. The water hole was white and brackish and tasted sour and made us vomit if we drank too much at one time, but it was all the water we had.

"If we chop Chan up, Old Henry can also carry his leftovers, too."

"If we cook him, the leftovers will last longer," Rogers volunteered.

It had taken us a long time to bridge the idea of eating

Chan. He was a friend, sort of, even if he was Chinese, but the details of how we were gonna do it were just emerging. Chop him up? Which one of us was gonna to do that? Then cook the parts? Or just put him on a spit and roast him, like a hog, before chopping him up?

Rogers had the best knife. A Bowie knife. Sharp as a razor. But he was squeamish; much more than me or Jameson.

"We should have asked Chan before he died. He woulda known how to do this."

"We could just bury him and let him be. Then take our chances."

"That would be the Christian thing to do."

"Chan wasn't a Christian."

"How do you know that?"

"Chinese are heathens. Everyone knows that."

Jameson shook his head. "Ground is hard as rock. It'll take us two days to bury him."

"If we just leave him, the vultures and coyotes will eat him, 'stead of us," I added.

"That'd be a waste."

Jameson sighed, "I say we chop him. Carve the meat off the bone. Just skip the hands and feet and ankles and everything above the neck."

"We gonna eat the organs?" Rogers asked.

"Well," Jameson said, musing out loud, "everyone says the liver of the buffalo tastes really good and good for you, too. And maybe the tongue. A lot of people like cow tongue."

"I ain't gonna eat no tongue."

"Do you think all of that will get us across this damned desert?" I asked.

"I estimate we have two hundred miles. If we make twenty miles a day, it'll take us ten days. If we only make ten, it'll take us twenty days. Gonna be touch and go, either way. Chan may or may not last. But we have ol' Henry as a back-up," Jameson said, talking to himself while he stared out into the night.

"So who's gonna chop him up?" Rogers asked.

I stood up and held out my hand. "Give me the knife."

Both men looked relieved. Rogers reluctantly handed it to me. It had an elegant feel to it. Well balanced. A knife that made you want to cut something.

They both turned away as I walked towards Chan. I swung around, slowly cocking my Colt revolver and shot them both in the back of the head before they could react.

I waited until the echo of the gunshots died out in the desert night, then said to ol' Henry, "Looks like it's you and me, old partner. I'll cook 'em, and you carry them."

Sweet Tooth

Ralph Hieb

Tuesday, February 11

The detectives walked to the corpse, located in an alley off a side street.

"I'm gonna say he exsanguinated," Detective Sergeant Jessica Gritt said, kneeling next to the body.

After a brief examination, Gritt stood, turned, and walked to her car. Reaching in, she leaned through the window and grabbed a camera.

Detective Thom Harris nudged his partner, Detective Rodney Tompkins. "What are you staring at?"

Tompkins nodded towards Gritt, bending through the car window, "Just admiring the scenery. Ever notice that killer body of hers?"

"Can't miss it," Harris replied. "Most of the starlets in Hollywood would kill for a figure like that."

Smiling, Gritt wondered if the conversation between her partners would change if they knew she could hear everything they said. She held the pose a moment longer before grabbing the camera.

They stopped talking when Gritt returned.

"This is the fifth victim in as many weeks," Gritt said, as she took pictures. *I need to find this perp.*

"All the victims have their necks ripped open and are found

somewhere around a candy shop or a dessert shop," Tompkins said. "I do like the smell of fresh donuts."

"Yeah, and they all seem to be overweight," Harris added, ignoring the mention of donuts.

"Just helping us fight the war on obesity?"

"Hey Gritt," Harris said. "Have you read what the news is calling this guy?"

"Yeah. The Cupid Killer. In honor of it being so close to Valentine's Day."

Gritt finished taking pictures and walked back to her car just as the coroner's van pulled up. Doc Fletcher stepped out.

"Why do bodies have to be found in the middle of the night?" he complained. Turning to Gritt he said, "I'll let you know when I'm done with him."

Doc Fletcher and his assistant loaded the victim into their van. People stood outside the police lines watching the departing vehicle, each giving their version of the crime. A few taking pictures with their cell phones.

"Think we better start with the crowd and see if any of them might have witnessed something," Harris said.

They set to work. Soon enough, one of the uniformed officers found someone, who said something strange. "Can you repeat what you told me?" the officer asked. Harris and Tompkins stood by with notebooks out and pens ready.

"It was kinda weird," said the witness. "The guy poured something on the other guy's neck just before he bit him. I saw that and made a beeline outta there. Then called you guys."

"Can you describe the assailant?" Tompkins asked.

"Yeah. Tall, long hair and a cape, like the kind Dracula wears."

"Anything else, maybe something distinguishing other than the cape?"

"He could run real fast."

"Nothing else?"

"Nope," the witness said, shaking his head.

"Thanks," Harris said. He reached into his pocket and produced a card. "We'll give you a call if we have any more questions. Here's my card in case you think of something else."

"Is there a reward for information? Do you need to give me a code number or something like that?" the witness asked.

"Just leave your name and contact information with one of the uniformed officers," Harris said and walked away.

Wednesday, February 12

"Did you find out anything?" Gritt asked, looking up from her desk back at the precinct squad room.

"Yeah, Dracula did it," Harris said. He and Tompkins explained the odd statements of the witness to Gritt.

"According to the M E, traces of honey were found around the torn area of the neck," Gritt said, almost knocking over the stack of case folders piled on the corner of her desk.

"I gotta clean this mess off before the captain sees it," she snapped. Looking up at Harris, who was sitting on a cleared corner of her desk. "Get your butt and coffee off of here before you spill it."

"Honey?" Thompson asked, ignoring Gritt's frustration. "What's the guy trying to do, flavor the blood?"

"I thought Dracula could only drink blood and nothing else," Harris said with a choked laugh, coffee cup held in both of his meaty hands.

"My guess is that we have a guy who thinks he's a vampire but doesn't like the taste of blood," Gritt said. "Therefore the honey."

"That could also explain the maple syrup we found on the dead girl by the bakery uptown," Harris said, looking at one of the other reports.

"It's starting to look like a regular sweet fest," Tompkins said. "Maple syrup, honey, chocolate syrup, confectionery sugar, raw sugar—what's next? Sugar cane?"

"We better find out who's doing this or the next victims

will be our jobs," Gritt said. Leaning forward in her chair, she answered her ringing phone. "Gritt speaking." She listened then put the phone back in its cradle. Standing, she said, "Our boy has done it again."

"Two in one week," Harris said. "We need to find this creep fast."

Definitely. Before people start to wonder if the name really fits him, Gritt thought.

"This one doesn't have any stuff smeared around the wound," Harris noted, bending close to the neck, even daring to sniff.

"If it weren't for the torn throat, I'd say we have a different killer," Gritt said. She stopped talking to answer her phone. "Yeah, send me the picture."

A minute later, she looked at the photo on her cell phone, then handed it to Harris, "Look at this."

"What are we looking at?" Harris asked, passing the phone along to Tompkins.

"That's an image of the depth of the bite marks," Gritt explained. "Seems our perp has fangs."

"So we really *are* after Dracula," Tompkins said.

"Looks that way," Gritt said.

"We better talk to that witness again. He might have seen more than he realizes," Harris said.

"Good idea," Tompkins said. "I'll go with you."

Tompkins and Harris headed for the witnesses' address while Gritt returned to the station, all of them determined to find an answer to their serial killer. Gritt ignored the flock of reporters shouting questions as her car left the scene.

Thursday, February 13

"Here." Tompkins handed Gritt a cup of coffee.

"Thanks," Gritt said, putting the cup on her desk. "Anything new from our witness?"

"He thinks the cape may have been dark blue on the inside," Harris answered.

"First thing tomorrow check with theatrical supply houses to see if anyone rented or purchased one with blue lining," she was looking at Harris.

"Need me to go with him?" Tompkins asked.

"No. I need you to check whether any theaters are doing a play where they are using costumes involving capes. Might as well eliminate the obvious."

After the two detectives left, Gritt sat at her desk, drumming her fingers on the wood. She picked up the now cold cup of coffee, walked to the break room, and dumped it in the sink.

Walking back, she kept asking herself the same question. *Why not a completely black cape?* Upon reaching her desk, she realized the coffee cup was still in her hand. She threw it in the wastebasket and sat down to start typing on her computer. A brief search brought up a site that catered to steampunk attire, where she found a cape matching the description. *I'll be damned. The guy's into steampunk. I know Jonathan is into this kind of thing. I'll have to call him and see if he's heard anything odd.*

Just then her phone rang.

"Gritt here," she answered, and listened to the voice on the other end. "On my way."

⌇⌇⌇

"The victim is a twenty-five-year-old male. Looks as if he put up a struggle, but was overmatched." The person speaking was a uniformed patrol officer. "I didn't know what to do. Witnesses said the person who did this grabbed the girl the man was with and took off down that alley. I called for backup."

"When the backup gets here, alert them that I went after him," Gritt said. Drawing her gun, she went down the alley.

Cautiously, she walked toward a broken section of fence and squeezed through, continuing past an overfull dumpster. She held her breath against the stench. Coming to a partially open metal door with the padlock torn from the hasp, she entered. At the far end of the hall, another door hung limply from rusted hinges.

She peeked around the corner to look out into the alley. To her right, the alley opened onto a busy street. Looking left, she saw the same thing. Shaking her head, she realized that the kidnapper and his victim where long gone.

"Which way did he head?" a uniform officer asked, coming up behind Gritt. More joined them.

"No idea. Take some men and start to canvas the area. Hopefully he left some clue to where he took her." Gritt said.

But their search proved fruitless. The perp was gone, as if he had never been.

Friday, February 14

"I heard you came close to catching the perp," Harris said to Gritt. They were back at the precinct squad room.

"Nowhere close. It's like looking for . . ." Gritt said, shaking her head exasperated.

"We're back to square one," Tompkins said. "I couldn't find anything about a cape with blue liner."

"I found plenty," Harris said. "It seems that about one hundred have been sold or rented in the last month. All of the rentals have been returned."

"Any with blood stains?" Gritt asked.

"They get dry-cleaned when returned. Any trace would be destroyed."

"I'm going home to sleep on this," Gritt said. "See you guys tonight."

Walking back to her apartment, Gritt's eye caught sight of a splotch on the sidewalk.

Bending over she examined it closely. Droplets of blood. Dipping her finger into the blood she raised it to her mouth. She attentively let the tip of her tongue taste it, *human*. Gritt looked around until she saw another drop. Walking to it, she searched some more and spied another. One drop led to another.

She followed the trail around to the rear of her building. It stopped in front of the locked door to the basement.

I need to get past this door, Gritt thought. *I need to get in before someone else is killed.*

Gripping the doorknob she twisted the knob slowly. Hearing the pin tumblers snap, she winced. *Damn things are making a racket.*

Opening the door, she found herself in a small room. Blood formed a small puddle just inside the door. More trailed off into the darkness.

Gritt followed the droplets further into the basement. They led to a staircase. With gun drawn, she waited a few seconds until her eyes adapted to the darkness. Then carefully proceeded down the steps into darkness, with every cell of her brain screaming for backup. This victim might be alive, or at least had been if it was the same one grabbed earlier. Slowly descending the steps, Gritt arrived at a rough concrete floor. She advanced across the open area to a door on the far side.

In the total darkness she had to step carefully. A crunch sounded from under her foot. She hesitated for a moment, and then reached out with her free hand to feel her way. Coming to a cross section in the hall, her eyes caught the dimness of light coming from under a door to her left. Edging her way along the hall she came to stand by the side of the door.

She was able to hear a faint whimpering coming from the other side. Placing her hand on the knob, she prepared to throw open the door.

"Jessica, please just open the door and enter," said a familiar voice. It was one she knew well.

Throwing open the door she stopped. Recognizing the black cape, leather vest, and derby hat with dark lens goggles strapped over its bill.

"Jonathan," Gritt yelled. "What are you doing?"

"I know how much you enjoyed sweets, and I've scoured the city until I found just the right one." He held the unconscious woman out toward Gritt.

She advanced gently, taking the woman into her arms.

"Well?" Jonathan asked.

Gritt lifted her face from the neck of the girl, and smiled showing her blood-covered fangs.

"I thought you would appreciate the taste, my love," Jonathan said. "Happy Valentine's Day."

Nana's Vegetable Soup

Carol L. Wright

The year I was in eighth grade, my piano teacher, Mrs. Cook, suggested I take pipe organ lessons. She assured me that learning the pipe organ was a guarantee of employment for life, and since hymns were already a part of my piano repertoire, it seemed like an easy transition.

Mrs. Cook had arranged for her students to use the organ at the Congregational church in the center of town to practice, and Nana lived only a couple of blocks away.

"This could work out great," Mom said. "You can go to Nana's after school, then spend an hour at the church, then go back to her house for dinner."

I wanted to take organ lessons, and I loved Nana, but when Mom suggested that I spend so many hours at her house, I was—I hate to admit it—afraid I would be bored. *Well,* I thought, *I could at least get a head start on my homework.*

So with a shiny, new key to the church entrusted to me, I was ready to begin.

Every Tuesday and Thursday after school, I walked the mile and a half into town to spend an hour with Nana before my late-afternoon practice time.

The walk was great fun during that New England autumn. I loved the deep blue skies and rustling through piles of leaves on warm, Indian-summer days. Nana and I found several ways to pass the time. She taught me to play cribbage, and, surprisingly, it turned out that we had a lot to talk about. Then, she would prepare a small dinner while I was at the church. I almost never got any homework done before Dad came to pick me up.

But that winter was especially cold. And girls had to wear skirts to school. Despite my hem-length woolen coat and my calf-high boots, I lost all feeling in my toes well before I reached Nana's house. Was playing the pipe organ really worth all this?

One cold, winter day, I trudged over snowy paths, crunched along icy sidewalks, and scaled crusted snow banks between school and Nana's. By the time I reached her door, my legs were numb. But I felt warmed by the smell of onions cooking in butter—the beginning of Nana's vegetable soup.

I ached for the comfort of the indoors, but my frozen hands inside stiff gloves couldn't turn the knob. So I knocked.

"You don't have to knock," she said greeting me with a squeeze, her faced creased in a broad smile. "Come in and warm up."

She took my coat and hung it up while I rubbed my legs to restore the feeling. As they thawed, I could finally sense how cold they had become.

"Come help me chop," Nana said, steering me toward the kitchen. She had already cut the carrots and potatoes. My job was the celery. "Make sure you keep the pieces as close to the same size as you can so they'll cook evenly," she admonished.

I took an apron from the hook, washed my hands, and set to work. The chopping took a while; it's hard getting those pieces uniform in size. Nana checked my work and pointed to a few too-large pieces I had overlooked.

When I got her "okay" wink and nod, I dumped the celery into the pot. Nana stirred it in with the onions and added carrots. Once they had a chance to soften, she added the other ingredients: beef broth, tomatoes, salt, pepper, parsley, soy sauce, Worcestershire sauce, paprika. There was no beef in her vegetable soup; that was a luxury Nana couldn't afford.

"Okay, now," she said, her tight, blue-white curls loosening in the humid kitchen. "Stir everything together—*slowly*—so that it's evenly mixed." I tried to stir slowly but still slopped some broth out of the pot. It sizzled and smoked on the stove. She arched a brow and handed me the sponge.

Under her watchful eye, I continued stirring until all was blended to her satisfaction. Wiping her hands on her apron, she said, "Wonderful. I'll put the kettle on, and we'll have some tea while the soup comes to a boil." Tea with Nana made me feel grown up, even though I added sugar—something she would *never* do.

By the time we finished our tea, the soup was boiling, and it was time to go to organ practice. But I rebelled at the thought of going back out into the wintry day.

"Do I have to go?" I used my best argument. "It's so cold in the church that it makes it hard to play." Then, when I thought she might relent, I hit her with what I was certain would be a winner. "I *could* just stay here, and we could play cribbage."

Nana hesitated, but shook her head. "Your parents are paying for your lessons. The least you can do is practice."

Darn it. Guilt. It worked every time.

"But," she continued, "I'll come with you if that will help."

I smiled.

Nana turned the heat down so the soup could simmer while we were gone. After wrapping ourselves up in coats, scarves, hats, and gloves, we walked in a gathering dusk past the post office, pharmacy, dry cleaner, hair dresser, bakery, and package/grocery store to the old, white-steepled church.

I unlocked the door, and together we went into the unheated sanctuary. We were out of the breezes, but in the still air it felt even colder than it had outside—like stepping into a freezer.

We could see our breath as I turned on the lights. I kept my coat on to play, but had to remove my scarf and gloves, and set my boots aside to put on my special organ shoes with a smooth sole and broad two-inch heels. Nana sat in a pew to listen as I fumbled my way through hymns and anthems. She endured my clumsy feet sliding along the foot pedals, the pauses to open or close stops a chord or two too late, and the dissonance caused by cold pipes slipping out of tune. Each error reverberated off the sanctuary walls. I could almost see the stained-glass saints cringe.

After I had tortured the organ long enough, I packed up my hymnal and sheet music, took off my organ shoes and slipped into my now cold boots.

"I always love hearing you play," Nana said as we started the walk home in the winter darkness. "You sound pretty good."

Bless her heart. I knew better. My fingers were too numb to be nimble, and my too-big feet never seemed to hit the right pedal, but I thanked her anyway.

On our way home, we stopped in at the bakery. The smell of breads, cakes, and pastries reminded me how long it had been since lunch. We picked up a baguette—warm from the oven. Even though I knew it wouldn't be warm by the time we got to Nana's, it would still have its delicious crust and soft center. Perfect with vegetable soup.

We could smell the soup before we opened the front door. I dashed into the kitchen to stir it, mixing the tomatoey bubbles on top with the vegetables beneath. Steam clouded my glasses and warmed my frozen cheeks.

"It's done, isn't it?" I asked Nana when she caught up with me.

She stirred it and made a face like it needed to simmer a bit more.

"Oh no. How much longer?" I tried not to whine.

"Just long enough for you to set the table," she said, tousling my hair.

I put our placemats on the old drop-leaf table, set out soup spoons and butter knives, and placed bowls onto dinner plates. Nana poured us drinks and laid out the bread and butter.

After she ladled the soup into bowls, and we said grace, I took a spoonful and blew on it, willing it to cool enough not to burn my tongue. I never waited long enough. But even with a scalded mouth, I could savor the blended flavors, enjoy the textures of tomatoes, carrots, potatoes—and uniformly cut celery. No meal could be better.

That spring I told Mrs. Cook that the pipe organ and I were parting ways. I'd find some other means of gainful employment when I grew up.

Nana didn't mind. "I'll guess from now on I'll just have to come over to your house to hear you play the piano," she said. That suited me fine.

But once the new school year started, I still stopped by Nana's a couple of days a week after school. And on cold winter afternoons we'd play cribbage and chat while her vegetable soup simmered on the stove.

Twenty-one Greens

JUDITH MEHL

Rose puttered in her farmhouse kitchen while the evening meal bubbled away. She'd spent the day combining herbal scents from the flowers she grew. The lavender always soothed. She pondered her addition of passion flower in the mix. Maybe she should change it because the flower served as an herbal sedative. She was so calm she practically floated around the kitchen, placing each jar carefully in the rack. Experimenting was the best part of her herbal business. And she loved it.

The sound of the rusty doorbell shattered the tranquility. Now with a sigh at the interruption, she removed her apron marked with dinner's beginnings and stowed it behind the pottery urn in the front hall.

She hustled across the creaky floorboards, comfortable with the old house groans and her day's work. She inched open the huge mahogany door. Her eyes widened at the twitchy young man tossing a bouquet of flowers back and forth between his hands. The bouquet settled in front of him like a shield. At a glance, she took in the mischievous grin and cherubic cheeks of Burt, the puzzling child of her neighbor from years ago. Today he looked the same, except for the lanky build and receding hairline.

"Hello, Mrs. Richards."

The young Burt, often left alone and needing comforting, had morphed into a troubled teen, tormenting townspeople, and their pets, and burning some of her herb fields. Her husband, Thomas, banned him from the property. But that was ten years ago.

Which Burt stood here?

He always could charm with that smile, even when developing his terrible teen years. She hesitated at a cheerful welcome, warring between her polar memories of the young and old Burt.

Her innate kindness prevailed, offering a polite greeting. "Burt? What brings you here?"

He shrugged, "Just came back to say hi."

Rose opened the door and motioned him in. A strong gust of wind announced a coming evening storm and pushed from behind to hurry them up the hall until she managed to slam the door.

Burt mumbled, "I heard your husband died. I'm sorry." He waved the paper-wrapped bouquet at her.

"Thank you," she said, motioning him toward the dining room. She looked at the bouquet, baffled. Maybe he was here to apologize for the past. She'd keep an open mind.

Moving to the sink in the kitchen, she glanced at the note quickly trying to absorb the cryptic message.

"A bouquet for you in remembrance of past loveliness. In the bud of life, you were as a camellia in and out, but you remembered me not when love was needed. What you have rendered you cannot right. Hopefully, life has been as rich as desired; nothing lasts forever."

Okay, the beginning referred to when he was young since, the camellia meant perfection and loveliness, and she certainly was kind to him when even his mother wasn't.

Still pondering the note she stripped the paper from the flowers, trimmed off the bottom leaves, and positioned them into a nearby vase.

"What you have rendered you cannot right." What does that mean? She should just ask him what's going on.

She studied the flowers again as she finished up. A foxglove in the center? Odd. And rosemary and forget-me-nots—didn't they imply remembrance? What on earth would he want her to remember? Him? The past?

She set the note aside to read later and turned to carry the vase back to the dining room. Her feet brushed past her old cat, Myrtle, cowering in the corner by the stove. Poor Myrtle. She was among the pets Burt teased mercilessly. At least the cat hadn't come out to hiss at him.

She placed the vase on the table and studied Burt while his back was turned. What did the note mean? Should she just ask him? Why was this making her so uncomfortable? Maybe she could just wait and see what he wanted.

He tapped the silver serving spoon from the table against his thigh as he stood looking at the family photos on the wall. There weren't many. Rose and her husband had no children, so she'd attempted to mother this boy from next door when he was young. There were no photos of Burt.

When young he'd beg for cookies and sit at the table with her. Together they'd planted herbs in the garden. She stared at the spoon moving rhythmically in his now large hand. He behaved so badly as he grew—stealing, knocking down her favorite plants before they bloomed, and painting graffiti on the shed.

Her mind flipped back and forth between the early good years and the scary teen years.

Yet, she couldn't ask, "Which Burt are you?" The one coming for cookies or the other one? She'd wait and try to be polite. He certainly had been so far. She smiled and circled her hand around the room.

"Doesn't this bring back the good times? All the dinners we shared with you and your mom. We haven't changed the décor much."

Burt turned, obviously startled to hear her right behind him.

He dropped the spoon onto the table with a clatter.

Why had he taken it? Giving him the benefit of the doubt, she decided it could be a nervous habit. She'd watch, and be wary.

The teen boy had seemed shattered that he was refused entry to their home back then. Shortly after, he and his mother left town. Rose and Thomas savored the peace.

She braced a hand on the edge of the table. "What did you mean in that note?"

He grinned, "Oh, I was just trying to revive old times. I added herbs to the flowers to show you I remembered some of what you taught me. Didn't you like my attempt at poetry?"

She paused. She hoped he'd changed. Maybe adulthood softened his edges. But those dark teen times . . . she masked her anxiety with a nod, passed him and mumbled, "I have to take something out of the oven. I'll be right back."

～⌒

He kept rubbing his eyebrows while he stared at the photo wall. With nowhere to go, he'd drifted with his friends until his mom had no choice but to slip them both out of town. What hellholes they slept in. It was all the Richards' fault. They'd snitched on him. The old man was dead, but this woman would pay. He hoped for an invite to dinner. He knew her food stash was endless. He and his best friend, Mark, stole from it often enough. Too bad Mark couldn't see him now. He'd seen her wrinkled brow when she entered the room. He'd probably have to beg for dinner. He'd kick up the smile.

Burt circled around the table, deep in thought. He'd timed this visit *perfectly*. After he made a complete turn around the table, he saw Rose open the oven. The scent of roasting chicken drifted under his nose. He stepped back as she entered the room and set down the platter of food.

"I sure remember your roast chicken. Best I ever had."

He saw her annoyance, but she pointed to the chair in front

of the placemat and cutlery and asked. "Stay for dinner?"

"Thank you. I sure would like to." She hurried back to the kitchen and returned with another place setting. Then his breath hissed between his teeth. His designated chair was far from where old Mr. Richards sat and ruled for years. She probably never let anyone sit there. But Burt took the given chair. Not good to tick her off now.

He smiled when she placed the salad bowl on the table. The gamble that chicken and dumplings were still the Friday night fare had paid off. He knew that Rose always served it with her famous twenty-greens salad. Every week, the same thing. The same scent of lovage came from the bowl in the center of the table tonight. He remembered it tasted like celery to him then, and his palate hadn't changed. He could hear her rave about the "nippy piquancy" of coriander like it was yesterday.

Sheesh! It was only lettuce. But now it served his purpose. Salad burnet was one of the old lady's favorites; so he knew that it would be there, and its cucumber-like taste would help hide any other odd flavors.

Rose settled into her chair and dished out the meal.

"What's with the herb farm these days?" Burt asked.

Rose reached for her napkin as she answered, giving a rundown on the latest additions.

He managed the delicate, yet crucial, question, though the fork almost fell from his sweaty hands. "How's that old ticker doing? Still on that heart medicine that crotchety Doc Simon gave you?"

"Why yes; how thoughtful of you to ask. My heart's holding," Rose said, her hands fluttering nervously. "Excuse me." Her chair stuttered backward and almost fell over at her abrupt rising.

Wow, that threw her off. Probably remembered I couldn't care less about her health, any more than that of cranky old Richards. The man deserved to die all those years ago. He hated me. Wish I'd had something to do with it.

"I'm sorry. I forgot the salad dressing." She scurried out.

Burt took a huge serving of the salad, then pulled a tiny packet from the front shirt pocket and slipped the mild green, slightly fuzzy leaves into the remaining salad in the bowl. He had just enough time to stir it in. *Now it's twenty-one greens.* He hid his malicious smirk with a mouthful of salad. Ugh. Bare greens were the worst. He should have shoveled in some chicken.

She returned with the creamy bacon dressing. "Dig in. Oh, I see, you already did. Well, you always loved my salads."

He forced a smile. *Always felt like puking at this meal. Mom practically beat me if I wasn't polite. I still remember those bitter greens—sure made my mouth pucker. I'll eat them cheerfully now since it'll be the last time.*

"Mr. Richards died when? I remember reading about it. Must have been, what? Twenty weeks ago? No, twenty-one, wasn't it?"

Rose's eyes widened, and he noticed she gagged a little on the salad. Was that terror he'd seen?

He looked down, trying not to notice. Looks like it flustered her though. Lately, all the memories of his childhood haunted him endlessly. He would wipe them out one at a time. This old bag was only the first.

He stuffed his mouth with steaming dumplings to keep the conversation brief. Then, like a chime in his head, the old lady started retelling the story of King James II. *Ugh! Not that old dead dude again.*

She kept going, not knowing what he was thinking. "King James felt any salad should contain at least thirty-five ingredients. Great idea, though I leave a lot of the root vegetables out. I like to stop at twenty. That's enough for me."

Well, she always did say those greens were the best part of her meal. He watched her eat the salad, in small, mincing bites. But she ate it all.

With a slight nudge, he centered the vase on the table. He glanced at it with smoldering glee as they ate, noting the fox-glove towering in the midst of the bouquet. Would she live long enough to realize its significance?

Marmalade

Headley Hauser

What, exactly is the attraction of marmalade? Pieces of orange peel floating in goo. Would plastic or metal filings become delectable if we could just find an appropriate sugary suspension?

Years ago, that great gourmand, Andy Griffith, espoused the philosophy that anything is "good" if accompanied by the proper salted cracker. (It does make you think twice about the quality of Aunt Bea's cooking.) It's this sort of thinking, (along with a formerly respectable Jell-O brand spokesperson's assertion that there's always room for cold gelatinous compounds) that, in my opinion, perpetuates marmalade in our society. But how does such a thing get started?

Origins are fuzzy things, but I'm willing to guess it went something like this. Sir Francis Drake returns to England after another successful pirating of a Spanish galleon. Among the purloined stores was a supply of oranges. By the time they reach England the oranges have gone bad, and the ship's cook throws them out. An adventurous domestic with missing teeth and uncontrollable red hair (they always look that way in the movies) salvages them from the trash heap and takes them home. She tries one and though it's rotting, it's still several degrees better than any food served in England. Recognizing that these little orange globes are the only things with "taste" she will ever encounter, she preserves every scrap in any way she can think of. Dutifully, recording her recipe (she also invented fruitcake, but I think others have dealt sufficiently that treat) she foists it on succeeding generations who in the rush of nostalgia and tradition ignore its overall lack of edibility.

In the final analysis, it's all Sir Francis Drake's fault. I was going to blame Sir Walter Raleigh, but I figured the tobacco industry has had it pretty rough lately, and he wasn't known for taking too many Spanish galleons. As a matter of fact, he was pretty much a wimp when it came to ship-to-ship combat in general. He'd just sit there smoking his pipe and passing the crumpets to Pocahontas.

Sir Francis Drake, on the other hand, was enthusiastic about the arts of murder, mayhem, and plunder. The kingdom of Spain pressured Queen Liz One to turn him over on countless occasions and to this day, he is banned from all the fashionable Iberian beaches and the Generalissimo Francisco Franco mausoleum gift-shop. Of course, Sir Francis has been dead for nearly four hundred years, so is incapable of obtaining the perfect tan and can haunt the gift-shop whenever he wishes.

It's just as well that Sir Francis has passed, for if he were alive today, he would be subject to the capricious vagaries that are the American Civil Court System. No dead queen with an inch and a half of cake makeup could protect him from a power so potent that it can take a murderer and make him give up his Heisman trophy.

"Sir Francis, do you know why you have been called before this court?"

"Well, I spent several years being a pirate. I killed countless Spanish sailors and scores of aboriginal people in the bargain. I made pirating fashionable and respectable among the lower strata of English nobility, which ushered in nearly three centuries of murder, mayhem, and plunder. (It also did quite a number on the hawking and jousting industries.) I also started some salacious rumors about Queen Elizabeth which led eventually to tabloid television."

Gasps and cries of "tabloid television!" echo throughout the courtroom.

"We'll discuss the tabloid television charge at a later date. You're here to answer for marmalade."

"What's marmalade?"

"A breakfast spread popular with English grandparents and Paddington Bear."

"I'm afraid I don't understand."

"Try some." The bailiff, who is an aspiring actor, hands Sir Frances a slice of toast with marmalade. He bows to the audience watching on Court TV.

"Hmm—a bit of flavor here. Like any good Englishman, I'm not used to that. I like the toasted bread idea. I do have one question, though."

"Yes, Sir Francis?"

Sir Francis appears as if he's not certain he wants an answer. "Just what are these stringy bits?"

The Widow Next Door

Marianne H. Donley

The stench of burning cheese awoke Neill Yates.

But the shouting, doors banging, trash cans clattering, and dogs barking kept him from going back to sleep. He stumbled from his bed, slammed his window shut, then pulled the drapes. Hard. He fell back in bed and squashed a pillow over his head. It didn't help.

What the hell is my neighbor doing at this ungodly hour of the morning?

He tossed the pillow on the floor and glared at the clock. Only four hours of sleep. He couldn't function on only fours hours of sleep.

Neill scanned his darkened room. *Where the blazes did I put the white noise machine?* Damn it, he wasn't supposed to need it here. His neighbor was an old widow. This whole neighborhood was supposed to be established, stuffed with nice quiet seniors.

He didn't care so much about nice, but he wanted quiet.

Ah-ha. He spotted the white noise machine on the top shelf of his bookcase. He yawned, then got out of bed again to set up the device. He tripped over the pillow he'd thrown on the floor, hitting his shoulder on the nightstand as he went down. He grabbed his shoulder and lay still for a beat, trying to decide if he were injured or annoyed at his clumsiness, when the blaring of an alarm interrupted his thoughts.

Is that a smoke detector going off? From next door? It sounds close enough to be coming from my house. He groaned. He knew the alarm and smell of burned cheese weren't his problems, but sleep would elude him until he checked. He threw the pillow back onto his bed and walked out of his bedroom.

He didn't get far. The open side windows in his living room gave him a great view of his neighbor's front yard. *What had Murry called her? Old Widow Raynes.*

How had he missed the fire department arriving?

Two fire trucks sat in front of the old lady's house, lights still strobing, doors open, but no firefighters around. He decided they must already be inside the house. Sure enough, the front screen door opened as he watched; several guys jogged across the porch and down the front steps. Neill leaned closer to the window. *Are they laughing?*

Yep, they turned back to the open door, laughed and waved at whoever stood there before getting into their truck, turning everything off, and driving away.

Okay. False alarm. He smacked his forehead. Of course—the smell. The poor old lady must have burned breakfast.

He glanced at his mantle clock. Just after seven. He'd call his buddy, Carl. He'd be out delivering his boxed breakfasts. Carl wouldn't mind brining one to Old Widow Raynes. She'd appreciate not having to cook for herself, and he wouldn't have to worry about her burning down her house his first day in the neighborhood.

He grabbed his cell and scrolled through his contacts. Breakfast arranged, he stretched and went back to bed. He had to be at his restaurant by three. He had prospective employees to interview, and the galleys of his new cookbook to correct.

He needed his sleep.

Old Widow Raynes.

Ellie Raynes stared at the label on the box in her hand, and then up at the man on the porch. He couldn't be much more than forty, a bit older than she was. He looked like an upscale waiter, dressed in all black except for the red logo on his breast pocket. The logo matched the design on the box she held. She shook her head. "I didn't order this."

"It's not for you. It's for old Widow Raynes." The guy winked at her. "Your grandma, right?"

"What?"

"Neill Yates, her new neighbor, called and arranged it. Evidently, she totally burned breakfast."

"What?"

He laughed. "Yeah, Neill said the stench was nasty. Did she tell you the fire department showed up?"

Ellie felt the heat rising from her back, up her neck and across her cheeks. *The nerve of that jerk next door. After the run-ins I've had with him the last few nights—now this? Old Widow Raynes.* And it wasn't her fault the blasted dish burned. She followed the recipe exactly as written—one hour at four hundred degrees. Too bad the idiot next door hadn't written the cookbook because then she would enjoy writing a scathing review and watching him eat the charred mess.

The guy in front of her shifted on his feet and interrupted her fantasy. He said, "Neill thought she would appreciate not having to make herself breakfast. I was wondering if you would . . ."

"I'm sorry," she interrupted while giving herself a mental slap. This wasn't his fault. He was just the delivery guy who was probably expecting a tip. "Let me put this down and get your tip."

"Oh, no," he said. He waved his hands back and forth, then took a step closer to her and rubbed his hair. "I'm not doing this well. I'm Carl McGraw. I own McGraw's." He pointed at the box she was holding. "We do boxed breakfasts and sit-down lunches. And well . . . I know you don't know me. But, I'd like to . . . Okay look, why don't you bring your granny to lunch on the house."

"My grandmother is on a Caribbean cruise and has been for the past two weeks." As she finished, she heard the pounding of giant teenage feet on hardwood stairs, so she knew Roy and Paige were finally awake. She noticed Carl look behind her with a puzzled frown on his face, so she figured the kids were behind her holding up the walls looking all bleary-eyed and wild-haired as they did most mornings. "How about I bring my kids?"

"Oh, my God. I'm sorry. You're married. Look bring your . . ."

"It's worse than that." She smiled at him. She knew it wasn't a friendly smile because he backed up. "My husband died ten years ago."

He shook his head as if he couldn't quite understand what she was talking about. She didn't say anything for a beat while he added up the evidence: missing granny, teenagers, and deceased husband. He looked at the box in her hands with *Old Widow Raynes* in bold black letters. He lost all color in his face and looked ill. "I'm sorry. Neill . . ."

"Tell Old Mr. Yates that Old Widow Raynes isn't interested in handouts." Ellie shoved the box back into his hands. "He told me last night what he does in *his* backyard is *his* business, not mine. So you tell him what's sauce for the goose is definitely sauce for the gander. I like burning breakfast. I'll probably do it again tomorrow."

She slammed the door before she could add something she didn't want her kids repeating.

⌇

When the oven-timer sounded, Ellie left the kids playing roller-hockey in the driveway and hurried inside. Too late. Smoke billowed from the oven like a malevolent, burnt-cheese-smelling genie and rushed towards the smoke detector. She climbed a kitchen chair to unhook the battery. The fool thing automatically connected to the fire department, and as much as the kids would enjoy the drama, she didn't want them showing up. Again.

She waved the smoke away from her face. *Damn.* She had cut the time the recipe called for by thirty minutes, and she had lowered the temperature to 375. What had gone wrong this time? Maybe the whole recipe was a bust?

Ellie climbed off the chair and turned off the oven. Then she turned on the fan over the stove and the ceiling fan in the family room, and opened the kitchen door and all the windows. Finally, she peeked at her dishes.

Okay, not what she imagined.

The filling had bubbled over the sides of both pans and missed the cookie sheet she had placed underneath them. She would have to clean the oven, but at least she had not burned another batch of shrimp enchiladas.

Using hot pad holders, she pulled the pans out one at a time and set them on the cooktop. The cheese looked golden brown. Now that the smoke had cleared, the red sauce bubbling in the corners sent the yummy aroma of chili powder and cumin all through the kitchen. She smiled. If the dishes tasted as good as they looked and smelled, they would both be keepers.

She took a few pictures, jotted down some notes while she could still remember her modifications, and then went to fetch some of the backyard hockey players to serve as taste-testing victims.

Before she took two steps, noise exploded in the front room. The sounds of the door slamming and roller-skating on hardwood floors and children yelling preceded the arrival of two girls.

"Mom, Mom, Mom," shouted Paige. Her face was bright red; her hair matted and sweaty.

Not to be left out of the commotion, Dory, her six-year-old niece hollered, "Aunt Ellie, the Hulk. Aunt Ellie, the Hulk."

"Skates off in the house," she said. When no one moved, she added, "Off. Now."

"But, Mom, this is an emergency." Paige took a deep shuddering breath and grabbed her arm. "You have to come."

The doorbell rang, and both kids jerked their heads toward the living room and back to her. Ellie read panic all over their faces.

"The Incredible Hulk." Dory wrapped her arms around Ellie's waist. She peeked at the front door. "He's going to smash Roy."

"Don't worry, Dory." Ellie closed her eyes and pinched the bridge of her nose. This was all Alexis's fault. She started calling the new neighbor "the incredible hunk" and the kids had misunderstood. Ellie had no intentions of setting them straight. She gave herself a mental shake and opened her eyes. The kids were still panicked, and the doorbell rang again, several sharp, quick bongs. "Is he on the front porch?"

The kids nodded as the door swung open, and there he was . . . the hulk, the hunk, the neighbor.

He looked different. She couldn't quite put her finger on it, sharper somehow and more intense. Up close, she understood why even the very-married Alexis took note. With dark hair tousled and that three-day scruffy beard look, any number of women were probably noticing. Not that she noticed. No, she absolutely was not noticing.

Right now, his eyes were closed, and he leaned against the door jamb as if it were the only thing in the world keeping him upright.

Ellie felt sorry for him. He looked as tired as she was, and then she remembered why she didn't sleep well last night, and the night before, too. Her sympathy meter took a dip below zero. "Is there something I can help you with, Mr. Yates?"

His eyes snapped open. He stood up straight. "Yes, I think one of the kids out there broke his leg."

⌒

Neill needed a detailed recipe with annotated pictures.

He'd expected to find a doddering old lady next door, not a curvy, thirty-something brunette who seemed to love kids and hate him. Serious contempt. He wasn't used to women hating him. He couldn't figure out what he had done. She didn't even know he'd yelled at the kids.

He wasn't looking forward to that conversation.

He'd offered to call 911, but she snapped at him, so he helped get the kid, Roy, into her SUV for the trip to the ER.

It was the least he could do, but he felt like a jerk.

He hadn't meant to scare the kids. Hell, two of the girls took off like he was a crazed troll. He wanted them to be quiet so he could get some sleep. He hadn't realized they were screaming because one of them was hurt.

He surveyed the area. All the kids who needed to be in the SUV were, and all the other kids sat on his neighbor's front lawn. He could feel their wide eyes on him as if they were waiting for him to grow devil horns and skewer them all with his pitchfork for breakfast.

The brunette ignored him. He wanted to ask her: Where the hell was Old Widow Raynes? And who are all these kids? And who the heck are you? Instead he asked, "Are you sure you don't want me to drive?"

"No, thank you, Mr. Yates. I think we have this under control." She turned to the gang sitting on the lawn. "Paige has her cell, so as soon as we know, she'll call. Okay, guys?"

"He's not in trouble?" one of them asked.

"Of course not, Zack. No one's in trouble." She smiled at each of the kids. "Go on home. We promise to call."

She didn't smile at him. But she did seem to be considering something. "Mr. Yates, we don't seem to have hit it off as neighbors, but could I ask you to check to see if I turned off my oven and then lock up my house?"

"Sure."

"Thank you."

"Should I check on your grandmother?"

She flashed him a look that made him feel she was sending

him to the principal's office for smoking in the bathroom. Okay. Grandma was off limits, so he asked, "Can you call me and let me know how he is?"

"I don't have your number on speed dial." She shook her head. "Sorry, that was rude. Give your number to Zack. He can text it to me."

"Okay, right. Go. Don't worry about your house. I'll take care of the house." He was babbling. One day in his new house and he was babbling. He watched the SUV until it turned the corner and then asked, "Which one of you is Zack?"

A skinny kid, all arms and legs, unfolded himself from the grass. "Me."

"Got a cell?"

"Yeah."

"Here's my number for you to text her."

"There's a please in that, right dude?"

"Yes. Please." Neill scrubbed his face while he counted to ten. "Please, text my number."

"Okay," Zack said. "Can we still have the enchiladas?"

"What enchiladas?"

"The ones Mrs. Raynes just made. She wants us to taste them. We even get to tell if we don't like them." Zack flashed him a charming grin. The boys and girls behind him were nodding and grinning as well. Neill tried to decide if he was being played when it hit him . . . the kid said Mrs. Raynes."

"Who lives in there?" He pointed to his neighbor's house. He had this itching feeling along the back of his neck that he wasn't going to like the answer.

"Roy and Paige, their mom, and Dory, and their aunt and uncle."

"That," he pointed the direction the SUV traveled, "was the aunt?" *Please let her be the aunt.*

"Dude. That was Mrs. Raynes."

"Where does the grandma live?"

"Don't know." Zack shrugged and looked at the other kids for help answering.

One of the girls raised her hand as if she were in school. He nodded at her.

"She used to live there," she said pointing to his house, "but now she's on a cruise."

Old Widow Raynes. Neill felt like his head was going to explode. Once it did, he would have to clean up the mess; then he was going to kill Murry. Just to make sure, he asked, "Is there a Mr. Raynes?"

The kids all shifted around suddenly uncomfortable. None of them would make eye contact with him. Finally, Zack said, "He's dead. Totally dead."

Neill walked through the Raynes' tidy living room and back to the kitchen. Her kitchen was small, but she'd used the space well, with double ovens, a gas cook-top, a big sink, and a fair amount of counter space. The white cabinets and a giant window over the sink made the room look open and bright. Herbs growing in shiny copper pots along the window sill added a cheerful note. He wanted to cook in this kitchen.

He looked out the back window. The kids were sitting, more or less quietly, waiting for him to bring them their food. God, he hoped they weren't playing him like Murry had with "Old Widow Raynes." He had a lot of making-up to do with his new neighbor. He didn't want to add to it by giving away her dinner.

She had turned the ovens off, but she had left the bottom one wide open. Cheese and sauce had bubbled over and made a nasty mess.

Not a huge mess, so it couldn't have been what he smelled this morning. It didn't look bad enough to attract the attention of the fire department. *Weird.*

He shut the oven door. On the counter by the cook-top, he found a stack of paper plates, plastic forks, and napkins next to two pans of enticing, cheesy enchiladas. He cut into one of the dishes and placed an enchilada on a plate. Out oozed tomatoes, onions, chilies, cilantro, and shrimp.

She'd made shrimp enchiladas, and hell if they didn't smell almost as good as his own.

Then he remembered the kids in the backyard waiting for food. He counted up the children, divided the enchiladas accordingly, and then called them to the kitchen door. Each kid took a plate, thanking him politely, before inhaling the food.

There was one enchilada left, so he dished it up and took a bite. Tangy, spicy, and good. Damn. She must have made her own red sauce. No way *this* was from a can.

He took another bite. They tasted like his shrimp enchiladas but with a little something extra. Another taste. What else had she put in the filling? A hint of garlic. Cumin. But that could have been from the red sauce. Ah ha, he had it now. Tomatillos. Why hadn't he thought of putting tomatillos in his shrimp enchiladas?

His shrimp enchiladas.

He looked down at his food. These were his shrimp enchiladas.

He put down the plate and fork and smacked his forehead. He was such an idiot. He was tired and overworked but how many times would he fall for Murry's BS? *Old Widow Raynes*, indeed. Murry had known exactly who his neighbor was, and he sold him the house anyway.

Neill had moved next door to Ellie Raynes, the blogger who wrote "Raynes Restaurant Reviews." The blogger who was making everyone crazy by suggesting how to improve their recipes. And for some reason, she hated him. So she would hate his restaurant. Hell. His cookbook. She was reviewing his cookbook.

He looked around the kitchen. There it was. Sitting there like a snake on the counter, the uncorrected galley of his new cookbook.

He walked over to the book. She bookmarked the recipe with a page of handwritten notes. In neat, precise, bold letters she had written: recipe wrong.

A bolt of anger straightened his spine. Then he remembered the fire department. He lifted her notes to check the cookbook.

He was so screwed.

When Ellie pulled into her driveway, she disrupted a mean game of roller-hockey.

"Look, Aunt Ellie, the Incredible Hulk is playing hockey with the guys." Dory kicked the back of her seat.

Ellie looked into her rearview mirror at her niece. "You shouldn't call him that, Dory."

"But mommy said . . ."

"Mommy was teasing, honey."

When the hockey kids and Neill Yates moved to the grass, Ellie drove down her long driveway and parked the car in the garage. The kids didn't wait for them to get out; they crowded around her SUV to see Roy, his bandaged foot, and his cool crutches. Her neighbor hung back as if he wasn't sure how welcome he would be.

"All right, guys," Ellie said. "Let's get Roy into the house. He has to rest for a while. You can all come back tomorrow."

"Can't we finish our hockey game?" Zack looked at Neill as if he hoped another adult would talk Ellie into letting them play.

"You heard her, Zack," Neill said. "We can finish the game tomorrow."

She nodded her thanks as the kids schlepped away, dragging hockey sticks behind them. She herded her kids toward the back door.

"Mrs. Raynes, can we talk for a few minutes?"

"I really need to get Roy settled."

He nodded. "Sure, but you need to know . . ."

"Mom, geeze," Roy said. "I'm fifteen. I don't need you to tuck me in. I can do it myself."

The doctor said it was a clean, simple break. But Ellie knew he was hurting, so she forgave his grumpiness. "Okay, kiddo. Get yourself settled. I'll be in to check on you."

"Mom." His voice was high and whiny.

"I'm checking for me, Roy. I just need to know you're okay."

He nodded and, with his crutches, plonked along the driveway to the back door. Paige and Dory followed him, chatting quietly.

"Is he okay?" Neill asked.

She nodded.

"Before I say anything else, you need to know I'm the chef and owner of 'After Five' and I saw the galley of my cookbook on your counter."

"Ah," she said. "Worried about your review."

"More than you know." He shoved his hands into the back pocket of his jeans.

"I guess you would have been nicer last night."

"I honestly have no idea what you're talking about."

Ellie gazed at him. He *did* look different in the daylight. She pushed the thought away and said, "When you had your wild housewarming party in your spa."

"I work at night."

"Is that what you call it?" She folded her arms and gave him one of her looks.

He didn't back down like most people did. "I'm the chef. I was at work until three in the morning."

"So, what? Last night your evil twin told me what he does in his backyard is his business, not mine?"

"Yep. Exactly. I have an evil twin." He pulled his wallet out of his pocket and took out a snapshot. "See. Here we are. His name is Murry."

She took the picture from him. Sure enough. Identical twins. She handed the photo back.

"I have a lot of other stuff to apologize for," he said.

"Like what?"

"The fire department this morning. I'm assuming that was your first batch of shrimp enchiladas. Major typo in the recipe. My entire fault."

"Okay."

"For believing Murry when he told me about 'Old Widow Raynes'."

"Okay, why would he tell you that?" she asked.

"Selling point for the house. I wanted a quiet neighborhood with lots of quiet, old people. I sleep most days." He rubbed his face. "Don't worry. I called a bunch of contractors about installing soundproofing."

"Okay," she said.

"And for yelling at your son when he was hurt. I'm sorry about that. I didn't mean to scare the kids. I wanted them to be quiet so I could sleep."

"That one might not be totally your fault." Ellie smiled. "Make sure you ask my sister-in-law to explain why the kids think you're the Incredible Hulk."

"You can't explain?"

"Not on your life."

He took a deep breath. "So, do you think we could pretend this whole day never happened?"

"Maybe," Ellie said.

"Hi. I'm Neill Yates. I just moved in next door."

"Hi, Neill. I'm Ellie Raynes. Welcome to the neighborhood."

He held out his hand, and Ellie took it. He smiled at her, and maybe just maybe, she noticed.

Preserves

Tracy Falenwolfe

Winner of the 2014 Bethlehem Writers Roundtable Short Story Award

Charles and Julia were the new couple on the block. They arrived on a cloudless, blue-skied day at the beginning of June, at a time when everyone on the street still visited newcomers to welcome them to the neighborhood.

The elderly widow across the way, while not much for conversation, offered a bowl of the largest, juiciest, most fragrant strawberries either of them had ever tasted, and the next spring sent one of her grandsons to the door clutching a plant in his fist, the roots kept moist with a wadded up soggy paper towel wrapped in a crumpled, well-worn piece of aluminum foil.

Dutifully, the couple planted the scrawny vine amongst the peas, beans, tomatoes, and lettuce in their very first garden, but it did not produce. The widow watched but did not offer advice. A smile creased her leathery face, but it didn't reach her eyes. She clutched a small bowl of berries to her chest and turned away.

The second summer fared better for Charles and Julia's vine. They collected one scant pint of small but delicious berries, and ate them standing in the garden, she in a pale yellow sundress, and he with one hand wrapped around her pregnant, swollen belly while the widow across the way looked on.

By the third summer, the berries were huge and sweet and tart and plentiful. Their aroma wafted on the breeze; their juices stained the baby's fingers. The couple didn't see the widow much that summer. They were busy with the baby and had another one on the way. They didn't realize the widow was so ill until her family gathered to say goodbye. They hadn't known her well, but they paid their respects, saddened by the loss, yet accepting the inevitable.

The couple had three more children over the years, and the strawberry vines multiplied as well, burgeoning with more velvety, luscious fruits than the young family could eat or share.

Julia's first batch of preserves didn't set up as she had hoped—the berries she'd used had all been ripe. But good preserves, she learned through trial and error, required some under-ripe fruits in the mix.

Making the preserves became a family affair. Together they would harvest the berries, scald the jars, and melt the paraffin. One of the children would cut squares of gingham with pinking shears, another would use gold cord to tie the cloth around the tops of the jars earmarked for Christmas gifts. The girls helped their mother with the secret mix.

Family, neighbors, and friends looked forward to the gifts. They served the mouthwatering, jewel-toned chunks over pound cake and ice cream, on toast and pancakes, in punches and daiquiris. Charles ate the sweet sticky preserves only one way: atop a buttery cracker, smeared with cream cheese, aside a cup of tea.

He was the gardener; his wife the cook. Year after year he tilled and weeded and fertilized. He anticipated as the vines flowered, and the green berries appeared. He taught the children to wait. And how to twist a ripe berry off the vine at the exact moment when it would make a soft pop, and the juicy flesh would be tender, but firm enough to withstand squeezing little fingers, and the fragrance would release and float in the air, and every fruit brimmed with the taste of warm sunshine.

There were ups and downs, but never a year without the preserves. As with fine wine, Charles differentiated the vintages on his palate. He could taste a dry year, a moist one, an abundant harvest, and a stingy yield. He appreciated them all, always on his crackers with his cream cheese, alongside his tea.

In the beginning, he had to ration. So many jars were set aside for gifts. Those that were left didn't last very long, and he had to wait months for the new batch. Maybe he hid one or two jars in the basement away from the kids and savored them in solitude, in secret, as he waited for another summer to roll around. But eventually he didn't have to.

The kids grew up and started their lives. The gift list dwindled, as long-time recipients aged and passed away or moved to warmer climates. Still, Charles tended the garden and Julia put up the preserves. They harvested the berries, and scalded the jars, and melted the paraffin together. They cut the cloth, and tied the squares to the tops of the jars, and reminisced.

The year things started to change, both the oldest and youngest came home for the summer. The oldest ate the berries, impressed to learn that Charles had never used chemicals to control pests. He explained he'd used companion planting, and some old wives tales that had worked for him instead, and pointed out that she'd known this all along as she'd been there from the start.

She had indeed, but she'd never thought of her father as an "organic" gardener. The youngest assured her that he wasn't, because his soil was not officially certified. When they left to go back to school, both refused to take preserves with them. "Too much sugar," they scoffed. "It's not safe to use paraffin to seal the jars," they agreed. "You'll give us botulism," they accused.

Julia was hurt. Charles was angry. But it was just a phase, they agreed. One day their offspring would remember their childhoods, the fun they'd all had, the joy the strawberries had brought them as a family. Charles knew this because he remembered everything every time he had his favorite snack.

There were fewer berries the next summer, and inexplicably so. Neither weather nor pests were to blame. It was almost as if the vine had grown fickle. But the berries the vine did offer were succulent and perfect, as they always were, as nature intended. And so Charles and Julia once again scalded the jars and melted the wax, and cut the squares of cloth.

Soon they met their first grandchild. A son of their son. An heir. His father had eaten strawberries since the time he could walk, but this child's mother forbade it. She had books and pamphlets and timelines, and more worries than she should. But while Charles harvested, nesting the berries in a large wicker basket, his grandson toddled behind. And if a few berries were missing at the end of his task, and if more fingers than his own were stained, he kept it to himself. The kid knew what he liked.

More grandchildren followed. Charles and Julia met them one by one. Each of them ate strawberries and smiled a surprised little smile after the first one of each year. Each of them learned to harvest and watched the preserves being made.

Then came the summer no one came home. They had vacations and tournaments and commitments. Other plans. Julia no longer helped with the harvest, but Charles set up a chair so she could watch. He dragged a crate into the garden so he could sit and pick berries because his knees were no longer what they used to be. The process was slow and arduous, but soon the basket was full, as always. The couple sat in the garden and ate strawberries, and remembered, each of them, the beginning. And then they were quiet for a very long while.

"It's time," Julia said, and Charles wiped a tear from his eye. He dug up a healthy plant and wrapped the roots in a moist paper towel, then took it across the way to the young couple who had just moved in.

The gifted vine wouldn't produce much the following year, Charles knew. But with a little tending, and a little patience, it would provide sweet, juicy berries for a lifetime.

Julia insisted on making the preserves that summer, though it was difficult for her. So much work for only eight small jars, but she enjoyed the task, and Charles enjoyed the results.

That winter was harder than most. When spring finally came, and the snow melted away, Charles discovered only part of his vines had survived. He tended and coddled, but that summer's harvest was slight. He glanced across the way, and to his surprise, saw bright red rubies scattered on the ground, and the gorgeous young couple plucking them up and feeding them to each other. Charles smiled to himself and remembered what was. And then he worried. He thought there'd be more time.

He sat on his crate and picked the plants clean while blinking the tears from his eyes. When his task was complete, there were only three jars to scald. Only three squares of gingham to cut.

The vines withered that summer. The scent of berries wafted on the air from across the way. The giggles and stained fingers seemed so far in the distance, but they made Julia happy. She sat in her rocker on the porch and nodded at Charles, her smile pained and thin, her delicate hand in his.

She slipped away that September as the last leaf yellowed. Later that day, the entire vine went brown and turned to dust. Though he couldn't explain it, Charles was not surprised.

The family gathered to say goodbye. Charles sat with them all—his four children, their husbands and wives, and the nine grandchildren they'd given him. Small talk dwindled. Hours passed into days, and it was time for his children to go.

He'd never been a man of many words, and couldn't imagine one existed to describe how he felt, so he pulled two jars of preserves and a tin of crackers out of the cupboard. There was a moment's hesitation, but no one complained about sugar or wax. His oldest daughter popped the lids on the jars. The youngest scraped off the paraffin. His sons retrieved the cream cheese and some little plates. The group ate and laughed and remembered. They hugged and cried and savored.

Soon the jars were empty, and the bags were packed. Charles stood on the porch and waved goodbye. He glanced across the way at the young family that didn't seem to notice him. Their garden flourished.

He went back inside and made his way downstairs. He pulled the last pint of preserves from its hiding place in the basement and blew off the dust. Upstairs, he sat in his recliner and held his treasure close to his heart. Days passed, but his grip never loosened. Though his mouth watered for the taste, he couldn't bring himself to pry off the lid, to scrape off the wax, to spill out what was inside. But he knew the sound he would hear if he did. The puff of fragrance he would inhale. The slight resistance he would feel as he drew the knife through the contents. He longed for the silky glide of the concoction over his tongue, but he wouldn't allow himself the pleasure.

He knew the work that went into tending the garden and making the preserves year after year. The love that went into each batch. He knew what he held in his hands wasn't just strawberries and sugar and pectin, but fifty years of his fondest memories, all in one little jar.

Metempsychosis

BERNADETTE DE COURCEY

Saturday night isn't usually my night to stay in. I'm a thirty-year-old woman; I don't really want to spend the evening sitting at home browsing the internet while eating a family portion of drive-through fried chicken and mashed potatoes with a side of healthful green beans. Even with all the windows open and the ceiling fans spinning and ticking, there is barely a breath of cool air in my two bedroom abode.

My residence looks like it is still waiting to grow up. Not too many mature adults have a pool table posing where the dining table should be. Empty beer bottles sit on the kitchen counter, unashamedly indicating that someone was drinking and that someone doesn't care. Not to mention the overflowing garbage and stuffed laundry hamper. I tend to save my cleaning energy for when I have company arriving.

It's not like my judgmental family would drop by without notice. Traveling a thousand miles takes a certain amount of planning. That was the best part about moving to New York- -leaving behind the worry that things done would embarrass my family. "A dog never shits in his own home," my study supervisor once said to offend the fourteen-year-old girl wearing a navy blue school uniform.

I remembered that incident because I have thought about the meaning of that saying many times since then. What exactly is it about certain memories that never fade, while others are impossible to recall? When did it all begin, at age nine with my first French kiss? Or age eleven with the first poetic letter from a friend of the family that thought I was cute? Maybe at age twelve when I accidentally discovered why some women give their shower heads names? It's all a blur now anyway. It didn't matter when it started, or at least that's not why I was facing one of the biggest decisions of my life.

Life is full of decisions, mistakes, alcoholics, abusers, loners, users, lifers, hopeless romantics, and the ever-present best friend that consistently disappears after being told, "No, it's not going to happen." Ambitious or just pretentious, either one works, or at least it does for everyone on *Access Hollywood.*

⸙

Sunday night was my usual delivery of sweet and sour pork, vegetable lo mein, three egg rolls, and the customary twelve-pack. Staying at home solo on Sunday was acceptable, even watching *Breaking Bad* alone was not questionable. Not exactly a show about happy families.

Was it more important to live a life privately that was true to oneself, or live publicly, trying to fit in where you would never belong? There's no real way of knowing; everyone has to choose the path that is right for them. Wanting to fit in can be self-destructive; don't believe that true genius beings walk amongst us comfortable and unnoticed. Nor do those who choose a life less mainstream.

Everyone's basic desire is to be happy. Food makes us happy when we are hungry, water when we are thirsty, sleep when we are tired, love when we are lonely. Ultimately we get up each day with the purpose of fulfilling our little and not-so-little desires to be well—happy. People who suffer depression have just lost the will to try to be happy. They are taking a break from trying; feeling unable to achieve what they desire, or they have lost something that their heart truly desires: a loved one, a job, or money. Whatever it is, it takes time to replace. My fortune cookie says, "Never give up. You're not a failure if you don't give up."

I ponder this. My hamster runs in his ball on the floor dropping feces on the carpet. It smells a little, so I plug in another Glade and pop another cap off my beer bottle.

I don't think I suffer from deep depression, but there is an undertone of disappointment running through my core on a daily basis. What my heart desires it can't have because I'm waiting for it to find me. I'm just waiting and hoping that the right decision will choose me, and in making it, happiness will come back. I try to imagine an alternative, but it would be settling for less than my true desire. I didn't even know what I wanted until I watched a movie one day and saw that it was me. I go and get another bottle to wash down the sweet and sour.

Monday already. Breakfast of champions. Three egg muffin things, a donut, and a large coffee, no sugar, just cream. "That will be thirteen-thirteen. Drive around." I am still stiff from sleeping on the couch. My mascara smudged below my eyes, not a good look. I hand over a twenty. "Thank you." She smiles and hands me my change. Then I take my coffee and brown bag. "Have a good day," she says to my closing window.

"I will have whatever kind of day I want," I mutter to myself.

How does one explain the Monday morning blues? Do we miss the lazy Sunday afternoon, or do we just lack delight in the dawn of a new day, a new week? I mean what could be better than a fresh new week? Last week wasn't so particularly amazing that I loathe saying goodbye to it. Nothing brought me closer to making my decision, and the weekend was pretty dreadful as Jason pleaded with me all Friday night to do the "right thing," and then my closest girlfriend got her feelings trampled on by her soon-to-be ex-boyfriend and was screening all of her calls, including mine. Therefore, I should be excited at the possibilities of completely new opportunities of messing up this week, but no, I am not.

If I choose what he wants, I shall no longer be free to do my job the way I like to do it. I shall once again be that inferior being, dreading work and tiptoeing around, hoping not to offend the Rottweiler boss.

Perhaps this is the turning point in my relationship; perhaps I have succeeded in removing the last person who believes in "the right thing" from my life. It's not that we are perfect together anyway. We have our moments of hot passion, but mostly we are pretty quiet together. I do ache to know that he still wants me. I have to know. Life has a way of hitting you square in the stomach sometimes. Just when I thought things were getting better, I made a duck's ass of everything. It all happened faster than the fall of a 747, but without the dramatic explosion and hours of media coverage. It's rather like falling over when no one is looking. It hurts, but no one notices.

Perception is reality, and as long as one perceives oneself as being okay, then one is okay. Right?

By Tuesday's foot-long meatball sub, the acceptance comes, not that we have any choice but to trudge along into the middle of the new week, replacing the blues from Monday with some heartburn. By Wednesday, I may have received some newer injuries over which to ponder while munching on French fries and chicken nuggets, and by the time I order nachos for lunch on Thursday, I shall already be anticipating Friday night beers and pizza.

Come to think of it, maybe the Monday morning blues are alcohol withdrawal blues. Quite possibly the removal of all alcohol from one's system can be quite anguishing. Those who have a drink a day are perhaps the ones with the least amount of blues over a lifetime of dumb fortune-cookie sayings. Now there's a new perception worth looking into!

It's Friday, and I'm taking the bus to meet Jason for pizza and beers. My arms are heavy. The man across from me is staring. Normally I would stare back, but today I feel he would see the dark inside me, so I stare at the empty Pepsi can on the floor that is rolling forward and back, trapped under the seat. I don't know how I will tell him. The ache hasn't gone away; the ache for his arms around me telling me everything will be okay. But I know it wouldn't have been okay. It would have been far from okay. I wasn't ready to be a mother, and I'm not sure that I ever will be.

Broken Heart Cakes

Terrie Daugherty

Racing out of Cora Zone's Lounge, Connie collapsed on a bench, her breath rasping in trembling sobs. As one hand clutched the metal arm, she hurriedly closed her woolen winter coat with the other, concealing the red velvet and satin of her low-cut dress. *Fitting for a "scarlet woman,"* she thought.

"Connie? Is that you? Are you okay?"

She looked up to see the familiar face of her friend, Amelia. "No, I'm not," Connie groaned. Then she burst into tears and plowed her fingers through the updo that cost her fifty dollars and an hour at the salon. "That bastard. That lying jerk never told me he was married. Here I was, trying to get on with my life, only to fall for the wrong man. Again."

"Oh, my God," Amelia said. She sat next to Connie and held her for a few moments as she cried. When her friend calmed down, Amelia said, "I know what could help. Rowena's having an Anti-Valentine's Day party at A Chalice of Healing. Wanna come?"

"If you think it's okay with Rowena," said Connie in a choked voice, fishing for a tissue in her purse.

"I know it will be. Other women will be there. Come on,

I'll give you a lift and take you home afterward."

"All right, I'd like that," Connie agreed. *At least the evening won't be wasted*, she thought, as they walked to the car.

Amelia drove to a quiet street where Rowena's small shop was located. It resembled a fairy-tale cottage. There Rowena sold herbs for beauty and cooking, books and literature, candles, music, and—it was rumored—spells.

"With this weather, I could use a good hot cup of her special herbal tea," Amelia said.

"For me, something stronger," Connie said.

In response to the doorbell, a middle-aged woman appeared. She wore her hair in a long, silver braid over her shoulder, and her kind, blue-grey eyes in a lightly-lined face broke into smiles at her guests. Her colorful, flowing skirt and oversized sweater made her exude a wise woman and fairy godmother all in one. Several mismatching necklaces rested on the front of her sweater.

"Hello, Amelia," Rowena said. "Connie, I thought you had a date."

"I did," Connie said, her body stiffening. She saw compassion fill Rowena's face.

"Well, you're welcome to join us." Rowena took their coats and led them into the living room, where the other women seated on the mix-and-match furniture. Connie recognized her friends: Karin, LaTasha, and Olivia.

Connie's heart stalled for a long moment when she saw Olivia. *If there's anything I don't need, it's her saying, "I told you so."* She couldn't stop the renewed flood of tears. Instantly the women gathered around to provide comfort.

"Are you okay?" Karin asked, sitting beside her and handing her tissues. All the women leaned forward.

Connie calmed down enough to sob out her story. "We were out to dinner and his wife confronted us at the restaurant."

The women gasped. "What happened when she saw you?" Karin asked, her hazel eyes concerned. "I see your beautiful updo is messed up."

"No, I did that. She threw a screaming fit until the staff

made her leave. Thank God Amelia came by."

"So, the asshole is married," Olivia said, handing Connie a glass of wine.

"Yeah, he is. Screw him. I won't be branded as the 'other woman' or a doormat." With that, Connie drained her glass.

"Whoa, girl," Olivia said and gave her a long look. "Just so you know, I had a feeling about this guy."

"In her defense, men can be experts at hiding things," Karin said. "Just like my ex-fiancé."

Rowena shook her head and pursed her mouth in concern. She crossed the thick rug to the hearth to add logs to the fire. She tossed a handful of herbs into the flames, which emitted an incense-like smell as warmth flooded the room. "We can start making Broken Heart Cakes. Get the ingredients, girls."

The other women echoed their agreement.

"What's Broken Heart Cake?" Connie asked.

"It's something I learned years ago from my grandmother," Rowena explained. "Everyone brought an ingredient."

"But I didn't bring anything," Connie said.

"That's perfectly fine," Rowena assured her, patting her shoulder and handing her a tissue. "You brought your tears, which will soon be dried." As the strains of Taylor Swift singing, "We Will Never Get Back Together," filled the air, Rowena set up bowls, measuring cups, spoons, and a mixer on the kitchen counter.

Connie followed everyone to the kitchen, putting on an apron Rowena loaned her. "Karin, I thought you were planning to be married. But you said, 'ex-fiancé'?"

"You got that right," Karin confided, pushing back her chin-length, brown curls and measuring out the correct amount of flour. As Connie sifted, Karin told her story. "I wanted children so much. Then I found out that he had a vasectomy. When I asked him, he admitted it, saying he didn't want kids linking us in case of a divorce. Apparently, he didn't think I'd break it off at the eleventh hour, but I did." She stepped back. "Your turn, Olivia."

Olivia broke the eggs with more force than necessary and whipped them to a frenzy. "You're lucky you got out," she said. "I caught my husband with his slut in our—our—bed!" She set the bowl aside. Her dark eyes blazed as her fist clenched over her wine glass until her long, red nails threatened to crunch into it. "Needless to say, I was livid. I stripped the bed, burned the sheets, and filed for divorce. I told him he could have the bed, but only after I'd spilled some of my perfume on the mattress." Giggles erupted from everyone. "He'll never forget me."

"So, he can't get rid of you unless he throws away the mattress," Karin said.

"Is that why you always warn us that we're getting into bad relationships?" Connie asked.

Olivia narrowed her eyes, but Connie caught the knowing look from Rowena. "Yes, I suppose it is," Olivia admitted. "I've gotta learn to let people make their own mistakes."

"We know you mean well, Olivia," Rowena said.

"I know, I'm sorry. It's just that I don't wanna see anyone else get hurt." Olivia's voice broke.

After letting that sink in, Rowena said, "Amelia, I understand you've got a new job."

"That, I do," Amelia said, adding the required amount of sugar. "I'm working at the hospital." She retrieved her new work ID from her purse to show everyone. "My so-called college sweetheart ended it after I graduated last June. He wanted me to be a stay-at-home mom. He thinks the only reason I went to college was to find a husband. Do you believe that?"

There was a chorus of groans.

"The next guy I find, I hope he won't force me into an ultimatum," Amelia added. "I'll just concentrate on my job and forget about him."

"Good for you," LaTasha said, as she poured milk. She purged her story as if regurgitating poison, her bronze lips tightened. "Would you believe I caught my husband in bed with another man? Of all the nerve. He wanted to sleep with both of us." Her smooth, cocoa-colored face was tense with revulsion.

Everyone gasped. Connie drew back as if recoiling from a foul odor. If any man suggested something like that, she'd run, not walk, away.

"What did you do about that?" Amelia asked.

"I told him he couldn't have us both and kicked him out on his ass."

Connie didn't feel so alone, after all. She was finding new strength and encouragement with her friends. But something else disturbed her as she poured herself another glass of wine.

"What's on your mind, Connie?" Karin asked. "You look very tense."

"I don't know if I want to tell," she said, feeling heat flood her cheeks.

"It's okay, there's no pressure," Rowena said. "You can talk whenever you want to and get it out of your system."

"We're all friends here," Olivia said. "Even if I do overstep a bit."

Connie looked up, a smile of agreement on her face.

"And what is said in this room will stay in this room, as agreed," Rowena added.

Connie drew a deep breath. "It's just that all my boyfriends have been one failure after another."

"Don't be so hard on yourself," Rowena said. "Give yourself time to recover and be alone. Don't leap into another relationship immediately after one ends. When the right man comes, you'll meet him."

Connie looked into her wine glass and slowly nodded her head. She had to admit, most of her relationships were on the rebound. It was time to learn to stand on her own two feet. "You're right," she said. "I'll take a break from dating and men for a while."

Rowena looked at each of the women. "You know, ladies, we must all learn from the experience and move on." She added her secret ingredient and stirred the batter before pouring it into the heart-shaped baking tins. Each woman wrote the name of her ex on a slip of paper and added it to the batter of her cake.

After the cakes were in the oven, Connie could feel the alcohol loosening her inhibitions. She started singing the next song, "I Will Survive," at the top of her voice, along with Gloria Gaynor. "You go, girl!" LaTasha grinned and joined her. Laughter erupted, easing her heartache.

They ate snacks and appetizers while the cakes baked and cooled. Rowena served her special herbal chamomile brew. They watched a chick flick about women blowing off their boyfriends.

After the movie, Rowena got out the ingredients for the frosting. Each woman frosted the Broken Heart cake with her ex's name.

"Now for the good part," Karin said, as they each got a luscious, frosted cake. They broke them open and threw the slips of paper with their exes' names into the fire, then bit into the rich, velvety sweetness. As Connie ate, she felt a power surge through her.

As the evening wound down, she said, "This was such fun. Thank you for bringing me here, Amelia. Olivia and Rowena, I'll think about what you said."

"Girlfriends need each other to help get over bad romances," Karin added.

Latasha apparently felt the same. "We'll conquer this, all of us," she said. She placed her hand out.

Each woman joined hands with her as if making a sacred pact. As the women hugged goodbye, Rowena smiled.

Bowled Over

COURTNEY ANNICCHIARICO

It happened when I was eight years old. I remember lying on the floor in my grandmother's living room, tucked under her coffee table, trying not to hear my mom crying in the kitchen. I don't remember if I had stepped on my grandmother's scale, or if I had brought home a note from my school nurse, but, somehow, my mom had found out what my weight was, and was devastated by the number. That's when I was put on my first diet. When I think back to my childhood after that point, I remember eating fat-free pudding while my brother and cousins ate ice cream, or fruit instead of cake, at birthday parties. I remember being taunted by my cousin with a bag of cookies, and my brother making good on his threat to stuff them up his nose when he didn't stop (that was every bit as cool to see as it sounds). Mostly, I remember feeling ashamed when I cheated.

But I had a secret weapon, possibly the only dam in the river of everyone's expectations that kept me from going under: my Gram and crunchy cheese curls.

That's right. Crunchy cheese curls, always served in the same green bowl and sometimes paired with jalapeno peppers eaten right out of the jar. It was our secret for years. As far as anyone else was concerned, my Gram was ever the honest southern lady, the stalwart matriarch, and I was the dutiful and chubby daughter/cousin/niece/sister ever on a diet. Week after week, Gram listened to my parents recite the list of snack foods I could have—veggies, fruit, corn cakes, carob—and solemnly promised to follow their instructions. As soon as they drove away, however, she'd pull out the bowl, and we'd sit around her kitchen table or curl up in her bed, scarfing down our illicit snack and, yes, licking our fingers clean (and brushing away tears if we were also eating peppers).

Gram knew I was very shy and nervous, and always second-guessing myself. I wasn't funny like my brother, athletic like one cousin, or thin like the other. The only talent I believed I had (and my mom wracked her brain to come up with it) was listening to others well. Plus, I had untreated OCD that I hid like dirty laundry. But once a week, Gram and I were co-conspirators, and every cheesy deep-fried crunch helped me drown out every other voice but my own.

Years passed, and I yo-yoed among a wide range of sizes. One diet always morphed into another. Everywhere I went, food was my enemy, and I acquired an encyclopedic knowledge of calories. Not at Gram's, though. If she caught me reading the label on the cheese curls bag, she'd just purse her lips, shake her permanently dyed black hair, and mutter "nonsense" or "never you mind." If I had wanted an apple, she would have given me one, I'm sure, but I never asked, and she never offered. I think it would have been offensive to what we had going if either of us had, because Gram's kitchen was the only place where I was already beautiful. Every time I ate my snack, it was as if I were saying, "I'm not going to change," and every time she refilled the bowl, she was responding, "I'd never ask you to."

Little wonder that the first poem I ever wrote, which won a classroom prize (a low-fat wafer monstrosity my teacher picked out especially for me), was about Gram and me sitting in her kitchen.

Gram, with those cheese curls and that bowl, saw me

through best friend break-ups, problems in school, problems at home. It was such a simple thing, a tiny act of acceptance and love wielded by a five-foot-nothing grandma, but I clung to it and her fiercely.

When I was sixteen, Gram was diagnosed with cancer. It was a terrible time, especially those last few weeks of in-home hospice care, when all the ladies in the family became our matriarch's caretakers. The image I remember most is that cheese curl bowl on her night stand, over-flowing with pharmacy bottles to help my mom and aunts control her pain. I remember staring at it, thinking I had to put it away so it would be ready for our next get together as soon as she got better. She was getting better, right? So, even though she didn't know it, Gram and that bowl helped me through a tough realization that day: that sanctuaries fall, and heroes sometimes die too soon.

So . . . you rebuild, and, I guess, the message in all of this is that you become that sanctuary for someone else. Today, more years later that I'd like to admit, I have two boys with issues of their own. To stand staunchly against the tide of their challenges, I pull out the cheese curl bowl (although now it's filled with mini white cheddar corn cakes—there's a lot of fat in cheese curls!) and we sit, licking our fingers, and wiping away the tears.

Natures of Origin

Diane Sismour

Trinity leads the five dignitaries through the lobby in preparation for this evening's event. She hides a smile when Christian's gaze meets hers, and watches as the tall Scandinavian's pupils dilate. His breath quickens as they approach. Somehow, he is able to maintain an impassive expression.

He opens the heavy mahogany doors to The Stoppers' dining area for them with ease, maintaining eye contact with her until they reach the threshold. She steps to the side and allows the guests to continue to the table. Once they move beyond the doorway, she nods to him to close the entrance. The sudden heat in his gaze almost has her forgetting the reason they consented to work such a late reservation on their night off. Dmitri promising to choose one of them as the restaurant's new sommelier after dinner service clinched the deal.

Trinity always enjoys the early days in a relationship: the constant tug of awareness; the intimate pleasures in the pre-dusk hours before rising; and the hoping she found someone for eternity. She glances past his chest, and down his tailored slacks, before reconnecting to his steady gaze.

He may not be the one for eternity, but he'll do for a century or so. Trinity flashes him a fang and winks before continuing with her duties. The result, she hears the skeleton key fumble against the door, belying his confident exterior.

The lock latches with a loud, metallic click as the bolt slides to secure the room. Conversations pause and heads turn towards the sound, but Christian's compelling tone is as reassuring as his smile. "No worries. We are giving you complete privacy."

The guests continue bantering and move to their seats at the circular, rustic table illuminated by candles in various-sized Chianti bottles. A large window displays the Manhattan skyline. The lights twinkle off the crystal as the nightlife continues below.

Dmitri, the restaurant's owner, chose a round table to reduce the posturing to head the festivities. He waits for the Portuguese representative to select a seat and holds the chair for her.

"Madame Philippe, you appear pale this evening. Are you well?" he asks.

"Just tired from the flight." A slight tremble reflects in the water as the woman lifts the glass to her mouth.

Trinity observes all the guests' nuances, as Dmitri charms the audience.

"Mister Altan, welcome back," she says.

"The pleasure is mine. Dining at our normal hour is a luxury on short stays," replies the Turkish appointee. "I've never tasted food quite like this served in my country."

For her to get the promotion to sommelier, there must be no interruptions tonight. Gaining the large apartment given with the position, along with the endless food supply is bringing out her competitive spirit. *Rah, rah for me,* she thought.

Dmitri glances at her as though he could read her mind before regaining control of the conversation. "We are happy to oblige you. Chef is anticipating your requests."

She imagines her favorite painting hanging on the entry wall to show her artistic taste just in case he is reading her thoughts. Unless he wants to leave his original Michelangelo . . . At her last thought, Dmitri's eyes widen, and he clears his throat. "Proceed."

Trinity hands the wine list to the eldest of the Mediterranean contingent. "Would you enjoy a bottle originating from your country, *monsieur?*"

"Merci." He hands her the menu and turns towards the Greek delegate, dismissing Trinity in a manner familiar to the privileged.

"Senior Verona, we have prepared *su aperitivo favorite.*"

"Gracias."

"Your servers will be with you shortly." Trinity smiles knowing the seamless way in which she handled the VIPs just scored her points with Dmitri. Her posture is straight, and her body relaxed, allowing the A-line skirt to sway as she walks to retrieve the bottles.

Christian follows her to the climate-controlled wine room. "I see you're feeling good about tonight," he says. Without her asking, he reaches for two bottles of Giuseppe Quintarelli Amarone reserve. "This goes well with Mediterranean."

"A floral red for Mediterranean, an excellent choice," she replies.

He places one in each of her hands, then leans towards her, invading the little space between them. He trails his fingers along her side, past the dip in her back, and settles with his thumb caressing her hip. "If I weren't gunning for the same job, I'd enjoy watching your ass shake all night long."

She makes the mistake of looking up. The rogue smile and daring glint in his eyes force her to focus on maintaining control. "Thank you, Christian. You are tempting, but this can't wait."

Trinity inhales deeply, drinking in the scent unique to him. The musky aroma floods her senses. Her breath quickens. She maintains control, barely.

He pulls her closer until their bodies make full contact. A pull within her wants nothing more than to forget the guests and react to him. She licks her lips, sliding her tongue along her teeth, testing her resolve.

He bends his head to kiss her, but instead whispers, "Don't drop the bottles."

In alarm, her eyes widen as she feels the neck slide from her hand.

Christian catches the wine as the top slips through her fingers. He raises an eyebrow and returns the Amarone to her.

Frustration at letting her guard down, and the embarrassment at doing exactly what he compelled her to do, makes her step away from him too fast. She backs into a rack of over two-hundred bottles, and the entire stack of Cabernet teeters before resettling on the crossed shelving.

Counting to ten won't be long enough to keep from clobbering him with the bottle. She closes her eyes. "When I open them, you'd better be gone."

She hears nothing but senses he left and opens her eyes to an empty room. Beside her are two more bottles of the vintage. *I can't lose my head over a man.*

She remembers the last man who lost his head over her. His dead eyes stared blankly from his severed head in the ditch. Dmitri helped her escape the village mob with an award winning performance by thanking them for rescuing her. His power to enthrall helped, too.

Trinity reenters the dining room, shows Monsieur Leroux the bottles, and receives the nod to continue opening the wine. She cuts the foil and pulls the cork. The cork's bottom is an even color and wet. If the bottom were dry, the wine would taste like vinegar.

She pours a sample in his goblet; the deep color coats the glass as he swirls. A fruity aroma permeates the air. The vintage is perfect, and she begins serving the first bottle before going through the same procedure for the second one.

The wait staff emerges with lollipop-frenched ribs, meat-filled empanadas, and meatballs in a spicy, white wine sauce with slices of crusty bread. Trinity nods to place the food amongst the guests and says, "Compliments of the chef, bon appetit."

When the diners appear satisfied, and her part in tonight's

plan successful, she joins Dmitri standing beside the kitchen's swinging doors. His face is unreadable.

"Problems selecting wine?" he asks.

"Nothing I can't handle."

"The apartment is yours to lose. Watch your step with him," warns Dmitri. He gestures for her to follow, weaving through the stainless steel sous chef tables.

He pauses before the chef. "Prepare the guests."

They continue along a short hallway. Just before entering his private quarters, Dmitri says, "Remember to trust your instincts when tasting, Trinity—color, legs, notes."

As Dmitri opened the door, Trinity notices Christian laying on the chaise, relaxed along the full chair with his feet crossed leisurely. When they enter the room, he stands. The white terrazzo floor glistens beneath his leather-clad feet. The large, unadorned windows behind him are black, the contemporary linear furniture is white, and slashes of scarlet in paintings and various sculptures accent the room.

Dmitri selects three goblets from a glass shelf. "Are we ready to start?"

"I'm ready if you are," she says.

Christian nods, "Yes, sir." His posture reflects the outcome, standing tall and confident.

"So we shall begin. There will be three tests. The winner becomes the sommelier."

"Are you returning to the old country, Dmitri? Is that why you're leaving Stoppers?" she asks.

He sighs. "Sadly, no. Alas, it's been centuries since I last saw Rome. A new restaurant, opening shortly in Seattle, requires my expertise. But soon. I'm tiring of this life."

"I will check on our guests, then return with the first tasting. Please have a seat at the bar," he says and leaves with the glasses.

Trinity climbs onto the high, wrought-iron stool with a cat-like grace. Her dress rises, showing more thigh as she crosses her legs. Her smile is demure, but she knows the effect she can evoke; men more worldly than Christian have succumbed to her charms.

He stands beside her. His gaze travels down to her strappy stilettos and burgundy-painted toes before making eye contact. "Even if you can't see your beauty, you are stunning."

She looks at him through lowered lashes. "I'm so happy you think so, but tonight we are competing for the same prize," she says, her voice low and sultry.

Christian moves closer. His lips brush against her ear as he whispers, "Let the game begin."

Dmitri enters the room holding the long stems in one hand, and a pitcher of water in the other. "Name the region of origin." He places them on the bar and slides the stemware forward. "Good luck." He lifts his glass, then swirls the amber liquid to silken the sides.

Trinity turns to face Christian. Her hand bumps into his arm as he's lifting the stemware to his mouth, and her glass drops, shattering on the floor. The liquid splashes across the terrazzo; the crimson against cut white marble is as abstract as the art in the room.

"Spain," says Christian without pause.

"Correct. There are paper towels beneath the bar sink. I'll get the next test," says Dmitri as he collects three new goblets.

Christian walks behind the bar as Trinity pulls the stools away from the mess. She collects the larger pieces of glass while he dabs the floor dry and wipes up the smaller shards. She throws the broken stemware into the trash and shakes her head in complete disappointment at sabotaging her efforts.

He tosses the soiled paper towels into the garbage and rinses his hands, drying them before pouring water into his goblet. "This is not how I wanted to win."

"You haven't won yet. Anything can happen . . . We just saw that."

Dmitri returns with the next offering. Once again, he places a glass before each of them, and he coats his goblet to release the notes.

She watches Christian hold his to reflect the merlot color in the light. Trinity notices the thin coating on the glass and sips hers without the usual olfactory ritual. The tannins burst over her tongue, and she knows the answer immediately. "Greek."

Dmitri smiles at her. "Correct." He leaves the room with three more crystal globes.

"That was quick," says Christian. He savors the remnants in the glass.

Trinity can't keep from smiling with that win while pouring water for them. "An even game, Christian."

"Do you care to make a wager?" he asks. "The loser has to clean up after the guests."

"You're on."

Dmitri enters with the final tasting. He places them in front of the contestants. "Good luck to both of you." He lifts the goblet to the light.

Trinity watches his expression turn dour. He removes a cell phone from his inner pocket and hits a number on speed dial. "Stop preparations immediately. Come to me for instructions."

Trinity lifts her glass to see what Dmitri had noticed. The color is off. She swirls the liquid and finds the coating weak. She takes a sip, and there is a bite to what should be a smooth finish. She knows the answer.

In a rush she says, "Madam Philippe is anemic."

"Congratulations, Trinity. Well done," says Dmitri. "And for guessing so acutely, I'll leave the Michelangelo."

Chef enters the room. "What would you like done with the guests?"

"Tomorrow's special, meatloaf. Except for the Portuguese. Feed her to the homeless."

Beside her, Christian slaps the granite in frustration. "Meatloaf! They have to be ground? I'll be here past dawn."

Trinity covers his hand with hers in reassurance. "A bet is a bet, but I wouldn't want you to scorch on your way home. I'll help you," she says with a smile.

How Sweet It Is

A. E. Decker

This morning, the truffles had been perfect.

No, not perfect, Marcel corrected himself. Never perfect. But he'd been satisfied with them, which amounted to almost the same thing. Now . . .

Now, a large, juicy fly sat atop each satiny brown dome. Fake flies—even Zachary Marten's pranks knew some bounds— made of raisins, with red icing-drop eyes and sugar wings.

Marcel braced his hands to either side of the tray, a litany of curses unspooling inside his head. Oh, no doubt the truffles still tasted of dark chocolate, butter, clove, and a hint of rum, but he'd die of shame long before he could bring himself to enter them in the Theobromancer's Guild prestigious Secret Ingredient competition.

Another batch wasted. Thank you, Zach. He sucked in a breath. Then, opening his eyes, he reached out, meaning to snap the truffles off the tray and discard them. When he touched the first one, the fly's wings quivered. The vibrations woke the next truffle in line, and suddenly the whole tray was buzzing. Marcel jumped back just as the thirty-six truffles rose in a dark cloud, hitting his hip against Zach's worktable.

The spell didn't last long. Just long enough for the truffles to disperse into every corner of the kitchen then drop out of the air, to either crack on the white floor tiles or roll under counters and behind cabinets. One made a bull's-eye splash into the mug of cold coffee he'd left sitting on the counter that morning.

Marcel took another breath, held it three seconds. It sat on his tongue, tasting of bitter chocolate and burnt sugar and honeyed nuts and cinnamon. Then, calmly, oh-so-very calmly, he went to his knees and began picking up truffles.

He was under the worktable, retrieving a cracked truffle, when the door connecting the kitchen to the Cocoa Dragon's storefront opened. Zachary Marten himself came strolling in, his golden dragon earring swinging jauntily. Marcel straightened hastily and banged his head on the table's underside.

"Just sold the last coconut creams," Zach announced. From the way the corner of his mouth quirked, Marcel knew he'd heard the *thump*.

"*Bon.*" Climbing to his feet, Marcel dropped a handful of reclaimed truffles in the discard box. *I won't rub my head, I won't rub my head. . . .*

"What've you got there?" asked Zach.

As if you don't know. Marcel gave in and rubbed his head.

Zach picked a truffle out of the box and held it to the fluorescent lights, turning it this way and that. "Flying fly truffles," he said, his mouth twitching from the strain of hiding his smirk. "I think you're onto a winner here, Lepret, but they need to be a little lumpier to get the full effect. You know, more like cr . . ."

"*Oui, merci.*" Marcel touched his gilded theobroma blossom pendant for strength. "Zachary, we are supposed to be partners in this competition. Why do you not only refuse to help, but also . . ."

"You're the Boy Wonder." Lounging back against the counter, Zach tossed the truffle from hand to hand. "I'd just get in your way."

Miraculously, Marcel managed not to throttle him. He turned away, gloved left hand clenching. *Get in the way.* Precisely what Zach had been doing, ever since Marcel arrived in Baltimore three weeks ago to prepare for the competition. The very first morning, someone (Zach) dribbled fish food into his initial batch of truffle filling.

And I tasted it, thought Marcel. He grimaced, his mouth puckering with the remembered dry, salty taste. If only he could choose his partner for the contest. But the rules stated that both members of a team must have studied under the same instructor. And since Master Terrence had only ever taken on two apprentices . . .

Zach stopped tossing the fly truffle and chomped into it. "Mm, delicious," he said, mouth full. "But less ginger next time, I think."

Grinning, he slapped Marcel on the shoulder. Then suddenly froze, grin dropping off his face. "Is that a spider?" he asked, jabbing a finger at a brown splotch on the marble countertop. Zach hated spiders.

Marcel looked. "Just some cocoa powder," he said.

"Ah, no problem." All good cheer again, Zach disappeared into the pantry, presumably to round up coconut milk, but from the rattling that ensued, he might just as well have decided to rearrange its entire contents alphabetically.

Marcel massaged his temples.

"Hello?"

Marcel whirled, nearly poking himself in the eye. He'd forgotten that Zach often left the Cocoa Dragon's rear door open to fan out the kitchen's heat. A dark-skinned, vaguely familiar, young woman stood rapping her knuckles against the door frame.

"Sorry," she said. "Didn't mean to startle you." Smiling, she held up a small sack. Its contents made a dry raindrop patter. "Casey asked me to bring these over. Espresso beans, for chocolate coating," she added when he continued staring in silence.

"Oh, of course," said Marcel. Casey FitzKinley, Zach's best friend and partner-in-crime. Casey sold the chocolate-coated beans at his café, Loki's Brew, and in return, Zach served his coffee at the Cocoa Dragon. Good advertising for both. "You are one of Casey's baristas, yes? Tracey?"

Her smile slipped a degree. "Tandi."

"Ah, pardon." Marcel often found people harder to remember than cocoa beans by region. People always gave him strange looks when he mentioned this.

She shrugged and the gold beads securing the ends of her many braids clicked together. "'Sokay. You were distracted when we were introduced. Taste-testing cocoa beans or something."

Oh, yes. Peruvian beans. The ones from the little southern plantation had been particularly rich and fruity. Quite memorable. Apparently more memorable than her face, although he did recall her beaded hair. And her blouse. It had been bright pink the last time, and not as low-cut as today's green.

Marcel cleared his throat. "Better put that sack on the counter instead of the worktable," he said, picking at his glove. Zach could be territorial about his worktable. He glanced towards the pantry, wondering if Zach would come out to say hello. But judging from the rhythmic noises issuing from behind the door, Marcel guessed that Zach had dumped all the cocoa beans he'd owned onto the floor and was now swimming in them.

When he looked back towards the counter, Tandi had already set down the sack of beans and was now picking up . . .

Oh, merde. "Wait," he said.

Too late. She bit into the fly truffle. "Oops, were those meant for sale?" She swallowed. "I can pay."

Marcel shook his head. "They're discards. Have as many as you like." He wasn't worried about dirt. The Cocoa Dragon's floor was washed every night; few plates were cleaner.

"Discards?" Tandi studied the truffle. "Why? They're really good. Did you make them?"

Marcel's cheeks warmed. She was paying particular attention to the raisin fly. *"Oui,"* he said. Going to a shelf, he took down a block of seventy-five percent Ecuadorian chocolate.

Beads rattled. He glanced back to see her shaking her head.

"You didn't do the fly," she said. "It's not your style."

My style? She knows about my chocolates? Marcel turned, swiping his hair out of his eyes; he'd been too busy recently to get it cut. Tandi leaned against the counter, seemingly casual except for the tension in her shoulders. Her gaze flicked to the pantry as another clatter arose from within.

"Is that Zach?" she asked.

"Oui."

"What's he doing in there?"

"Je ne sais pas."

She held up a truffle. "The fly's his doing, isn't it?"

Marcel huffed. *"Oui,"* he said. Such a relief to say it aloud. "I left them there to cool this morning, and when I returned . . ."

"But Zach's been at Loki's Brew all morning," said Tandi.

". . . the truffles were . . . eh?"

"Zach just left Casey recently," she said. "I had to run after because he forgot those, you see." She nodded towards the espresso beans. "When did you finish the truffles?"

"About . . . eight-forty?" Frowning, Marcel set the Ecuadorian chocolate on the chopping block. His memories of his morning's activities were surprisingly fuzzy. Had he gone to the market after finishing them? Or was it just for a walk?

"He was definitely at Loki's Brew then," said Tandi.

Pursing his lips, Marcel chopped steadily.

"Or could he have used magic to do it?" she asked.

Marcel almost chopped his thumb off. "What did you say?" he asked, spinning around. Tandi's eyes widened. She clapped a hand over her mouth. The clock on the far wall counted off the seconds. Every *tick* struck Marcel's nerves like a small hammer. How could she know? Only a couple hundred people knew of theobromancy's existence. Theirs was a secret art.

Tandi dropped her hand to her lap. Her other hand folded over it. "I know you can do magic with chocolate," she said, staring down at her entwined fingers. "I heard Zach and Casey talking about it." She met his gaze. "Don't worry. I haven't told anyone."

But Zach should never have told Casey in the first place. The Guild had rules. Marcel could all but hear the *snap* of the last straw on his back as he strode to the pantry and rapped on the door.

It swung open. "Yeah?" said Zach, emerging with two cans of coconut milk and an innocent smile. "Oh, hey," he said, spotting Tandi at the counter. "Did you bring the espresso beans?"

"Right here," she said, lifting a corner of the sack.

"She knows about theobromancy," said Marcel, standing in Zach's path, arms akimbo.

Zach shrugged. "Casey must've told her. Bad Casey. I'll spank him later."

Marcel glared, and Zach rolled his eyes. "That was a joke, Lepret. Casey and I have been friends for fifteen years. Of course, he knows about us Theos. Master Terrence cleared it."

"He did?" The air whooshed out of Marcel's lungs.

Zach nodded. "Yeah. Can I make the coconut creams now?" He made to brush past Marcel.

"Why are you doing this?" Marcel burst out.

Zach stepped back, tilted his head. Nearly said: *"Doing what?"* Marcel saw it on his lips. But perhaps he sensed the dangerously thin ice beneath him. "Is this about those fly truffles?" he asked.

"I'd never make such things," said Marcel.

Zach rubbed his mouth. "Aren't you taking this stupid competition too seriously?"

Marcel flung up his hands. *All* Theos—save for Zach—took the Secret Ingredient competition seriously. The victors got to sit on the Guild Council for the next year and influence all decisions.

You'd think Zach would want to win just for the chance to flick spitballs at the other council members during meetings, Marcel thought, glowering. "Even if you do not wish to help, why must you . . ."

"Hinder?" suggested Zach, when Marcel's grasp of English temporarily abandoned him.

"Exactement. Merci!"

"But I didn't."

"Eh?"

"I didn't," said Zach, staring straight into Marcel's eyes. "My word on it."

"Your sworn word?" Marcel challenged.

Sighing, Zach set the cans of coconut milk on the work-table, *click, click,* and pulled his gilded theobroma flower from under his shirt. Taking up a paring knife, he nicked the bony protrusion of his left wrist.

"I did not sabotage your truffles this morning," he said and touched his theobroma to the drop of blood that welled up.

"Or add that fish food to my filling?" Marcel added.

"Or that."

"Or . . ."

"Or any of it," said Zach. "On my word as a Theo, I haven't sabotaged any of your truffles since you came to Maryland."

His gilded theobroma neither wilted nor tarnished.

Merde. Marcel sagged against the counter.

"Am I absolved?" asked Zach. His lips twitched.

Marcel squeezed his eyes shut. "You're absolved," he gritted.

"Good." Picking up the cans of coconut milk, Zach banged them down on the counter in front of Marcel. "As your penance for accusing me, you can make the coconut creams."

A thousand hot, bile-tasting responses boiled up. "Very well," Marcel said, swallowing them down.

"Excellent." Zach slapped his back. "I'll go see how Alice is coping with the customers." He strode out, earring gleaming, ponytail swishing.

The wall clock's ticks resembled muffled sniggers. Marcel stared at the dusting of cocoa powder coating the countertop. After a moment, he began doodling in it.

Tandi broke the silence. "You don't believe him, do you?" she asked.

"The flower would've wilted if he lied." He glanced sidelong at her. Why hadn't she returned to Loki's Brew?

"Shouldn't you . . ." he began.

"I think he . . ." she started.

Their words tangled. They both stopped, looked at each other, waited. After a few seconds, Tandi laughed. "You first."

Marcel paused. Now that he thought about it, asking: "Shouldn't you be getting back to the café?" seemed impolite. Trouble was, he couldn't think of anything else to say.

She watched him, eyes wide and expectant. Her fingers toyed with a golden bead on the end of a braid. Marcel's cheeks burned. Noticing his gloved hand was still doodling in the cocoa powder, he hid it beneath the counter. "I best get to work on the *crème au coconut,*" he muttered.

"Screw the coconut creams," she replied. His mouth fell open, but she went on without missing a beat. "Zach ruined your truffles, didn't he? Let him do his work."

"He swore he didn't." Marcel picked at his glove. "He couldn't have been lying."

"That doesn't mean he isn't responsible somehow." Tandi moved her stool closer. She smelled of coffee, with a hint of violet. A gold chain, bright as the beads in her hair, encircled her neck and plunged into the depths of her blouse.

Clearing his throat, Marcel averted his gaze.

"Or could someone else have put the flies on your truffles?"

Marcel shook his head. "The only other Theo in Maryland right now is Alice, and such pranks are not her," he flashed a smile, "style."

"Yeah, I can't see her doing it." Tandi brushed back her hair with a tinkle of beads. "She probably gets her fill of tricks, being married to Zach." She was quiet a moment, tapping her green-painted nails against the counter. "I suppose he could've put her up to it."

"*Non.*" Marcel realized he was doodling in the cocoa again. Annoyed, he sat on his hand. "Alice is participating in the Secret Ingredient competition too. She and her partner would be disqualified if she tampered with my—I mean Zach's and my—entry."

"Wait, wait." Tandi leaned forward. Her chain slid along her brown skin, sparkling. "Zach's your teammate? Why would he sabotage his entry?"

Marcel laughed without humor. "My presenting the Guild with truffles that look like lumps of *merde* topped with flies would be victory enough for Zach. He thinks the Guild is a bunch of--how do you say?—relics."

Tandi put her hand over his. Not the gloved one, or he might have flinched away. "Doesn't he care about your feelings?" she asked.

The past three weeks in Maryland, trying to concoct a new and intriguing clove-based recipe all on his own—no worse, stymied at every turn—raced over Marcel. Suddenly exhausted, he propped an elbow on the counter. "Zach considers me the Guild's pet," he said into his palm. "Annoying me is as good as upsetting them."

Tandi frowned. "What a jerk."

"Sometimes." Sighing, Marcel stood, his hand sliding from under hers. "Might as well make the coconut creams," he said.

"I still say, let Zach do it." Tandi took another truffle, picked off the fly and bit into it. After a moment of thoughtful chewing, she put the fly in her mouth along with the rest of the truffle.

"I enjoy working," he replied, switching on the tempering machine. *Might as well clean the counter before I get started,* he thought and picked up his coffee mug.

It shook in his hand. The three inches of remaining liquid splashed against the sides, a few drops arching up over the mug's rim to dampen his glove.

"Hein?" cried Marcel, dropping the mug. It fell to the counter and rolled, fetching up against its handle. Coffee puddled on the counter.

The mug rattled against the counter. Tandi jumped off her stool and joined him in pressing against the worktable. A wisp of her coffee-and-violet scent wafted over Marcel. Shoulder-to-shoulder, they watched as an acorn-sized fly crept out of the mug, a tiny, shrunken truffle dangling between its six legs.

"Ew." Tandi's face twisted.

Marcel agreed. The larger flies were, the more disgusting they became—and he could swear this one was still growing. It vibrated its wings then took off, buzzing three feet above his head.

"Oust!" he said, swatting at it. His hand missed it by a good six inches, but that was all right. He feared it might burst if he struck it.

It answered with a derisive buzz. Marcel sidled around the worktable and the fly followed, maintaining its distance over his head. Was that the game, then? Keep the thing hanging over him until he got annoyed enough to swat it?

"More of Zach's handiwork?" asked Tandi, watching the fly.

"I'm sure he'd deny it," said Marcel. The fly suddenly swooped down, as if intending to settle in his hair. But even as he cringed, it reversed direction, returning to its sentry position.

It was definitely growing. Maybe it would burst even if he didn't swat it.

"I'll get it," said Tandi, stepping onto a chair. One hand steadied her against the back while the other touched her chest.

"No," he said. He motioned her down. This was between him and Zach; he wouldn't have her getting drenched in whatever yuck the thing was filled with.

Tandi paused, her foot still on the seat of the chair. She looked from him to the fly. "Can you stop it with your chocolate magic?"

He spread his hands. "This is Zach's kitchen. For another Theo to work magic in it without permission is against Guild rules."

Oh, so that was the game. He could either use theobromancy to stop the fly, or he could obey Guild law and wait for the fly to burst and drench him. Either way, Zach won.

The fly bloated to the size of a walnut. Its slimy gray-black sides gleamed, looking uncomfortably tight.

"Marcel."

Marcel took his eyes off the fly long enough to focus on

Tandi. He hadn't introduced himself this morning, he realized. How rude. She'd remembered his name from their last encounter while he'd recalled nothing but her beads and the color of her blouse. *"Oui?"*

"Screw the Guild, too."

But if I use theobromancy in Zach's domain, he'll tell the Guild. I'll be disqualified, reprimanded, perhaps even demoted.

The fly swooped again. Its red eyes, swollen along with the rest of it, gleamed like soggy gumdrops.

Tandi was right. Screw the Guild and Zach, too.

Marcel lifted his left hand, its gloved fingertips coated in Peruvian cocoa, the palm streaked with Ecuadorian seventy-five percent chocolate from his earlier chopping. The gilded theobroma under his shirt warmed.

Ecuadorian chocolate peeled off his gloved palm to form a shiny dark teardrop shape. Cocoa whirled off his fingertips, separating into eight distinct sections which thinned into long, jointed legs that attached themselves to the chocolate teardrop. The finished creation clicked its mandibles.

Marcel smiled. He could've sworn the fly's gumdrop eyes widened an instant before the chocolate spider leapt off his hand and caught it neatly in its forelegs. The spider's jump took both it and the captured fly onto the counter, where the spider busily wrapped the fly in a tangle of spun sugar and dragged it off behind the chopping block for a quiet talk.

"Wow!"

Tandi's eyes shone. "I can't wait until . . . I wish I could do stuff like that," she said.

The gold chain around her neck glittered. She'd touched her chest while climbing onto the chair.

Pursing his lips, Marcel picked the coffee mug off the counter and sniffed its contents. The lush, bitter-floral pungence of strong coffee filled his nostrils.

Loki's Brew coffee, from Casey's shop. He'd been drinking it every morning since coming to Maryland.

"What is on your necklace?" he asked Tandi. "The ornament, I mean. It's down your blouse." He smacked his forehead. "I mean, bien, I mean I can't see it."

Her grin remained in place, looking like it was glued. "Oh, it's just a gemstone," she said, clasping the chain. "My birthstone."

Marcel puffed out his cheeks. "It's a gilded coffee flower, isn't it?"

Her smile remained fixed maybe ten seconds longer. Then: "No," she said with a sigh. "It's just a gilded coffee bean." She drew it out. "I'm only an apprentice Arabicacerer. That's coffee wizard to you."

He looked at the tiny golden lump sparkling on her palm. "Casey's apprentice."

"Yes." A world of meaning lurked in her grimace.

The door to the Cocoa Dragon's storefront swung open. Zach swaggered in, visibly fighting back a smirk. Marcel wondered if he'd been out front, chatting with the customers, all senses alert for the slightest trace of theobromancy being worked in the back.

"What's been going on here?" he asked. Without waiting for an answer, he took out his theobroma and dipped it into the specks of cocoa remaining on the counter. The flower's petals glowed with a pale, rosy aura. Now smiling broadly, Zach turned to Marcel, who'd watched the whole charade, arms folded across his chest.

"You've used unlicensed theobromancy here," said Zach.

"And Casey's been using coffee magic," retorted Marcel. "With your permission, of course."

Zach's smiled dimmed then widened again. "You figured it out."

"He's been enchanting my coffee so I'd sabotage myself." Marcel shook his head at the simplicity of the scheme. No wonder he'd had such trouble remembering how he spent his mornings.

Zach drew himself into an unearned attitude of offended dignity. "Possibly," he said. "I don't ask a man for the tricks of his trade. Anyway, you still used magic in my kitchen without permission."

"*Oui.*" Marcel snapped his fingers and the spider scuttled from behind the chopping block and jumped into his hand. "Used magic to create this."

In a movement any gymnast would've envied, Zach leapt backward onto the worktable. Saying he "hated spiders" was something of an understatement.

"Getitout, getitout, getitout!" he yelled, white-eyed and hugging himself.

"This? But it's only a spell." Marcel let the spider run up his arm. "It'll only last a couple of hours." He stroked its back. "Do you know, I believe I'll miss it. Perhaps I should visit a pet shop and see if they have any of those big ones for sale. What are they called?"

"Tarantulas," called Tandi with cheerful malice.

"You wouldn't dare," said Zach between his teeth. "This is my kitchen."

Marcel put on his wide-eyed "perfect student" expression, the one he knew made Zach's jaw clench. "But it isn't like I'd be using magic in your kitchen. And spiders are helpful. They eat flies and other pests."

Zach glowered. "Lepret . . ."

"Actually, I needn't buy a tarantula," said Marcel thoughtfully. "An hour's walk every morning, looking under leaves . . . I could probably find five or six spiders every day."

Zach leveled a finger. "If I tell the Guild you used magic in my kitchen, you'll find yourself disqualified and back in New York by tomorrow."

Their gazes locked. Inwardly, Marcel felt as if he stood on a pile of sugar that kept sliding away from under him. Defying the Guild. Cheeking Zach. Did he really expect to get away with this?

"Hey, Zach?" Tandi's call drew both their attentions. She leaned her elbows on the counter, her gilded coffee bean swinging from her neck, alternately flashing and dimming in the overhead light. "Not everyone lives in New York. You could get Marcel disqualified and still find spiders turning up in your kitchen."

Zach stared at her. Then Marcel. Back to Tandi. All at once, he tossed up his hands. "All right," he said. "I'll tell Casey to stop enchanting your coffee."

Marcel smiled. "Thank you, Zachary Marten." He folded his hand around the chocolate spider and put it in his pocket. Scowling, Zach climbed down off the worktable.

"You really helped with the truffles," Marcel added as he stalked towards the front room.

Zach stopped, hand on the door.

Marcel looked at Tandi. "They tasted better with the raisins, didn't they?"

She considered. "Yes. They did."

"I'll try adding them to the filling next time then," he said. "Thank you, Zach."

"You're taking this stupid competition far too seriously," said Zach, staring at the door.

Marcel spread his hands. "All I've ever wanted is to be a top-class Theobromancer."

Zach turned just enough so he could meet Marcel's gaze without torquing his head over his shoulder. His dark eyes were sad. "The Guild already believes you are," he said. "Much more talented than me."

Marcel looked down. Picked at the back of his glove. The swinging door creaked. Then Zach's voice came again.

"Congratulations on defying Guild law, by the way," he said. "There may be hope for you yet, Lepret."

The door clicked shut. "He's right," said Marcel to his glove. "I broke Guild rule. Am I worthy of sitting on the council, even if I can win the competition?"

Tandi sighed. He looked up to see her watching him. "You know, Zach has a point," she said. "You can take rules a little too seriously." Reclaiming her stool, she crossed her legs. "Didn't you wonder why I hung around here instead of going back to the café?" She toyed with a beaded braid. Her gilded bean glinted against the green backdrop of her blouse. It was quite a nice blouse: silk, with lace. Fancier than what you'd expect a barista to wear to work.

"I'm a little slow, but . . ." Damn his hair! He brushed it out of his eyes again. "I think I've figured it out."

Tandi's hand stilled on her braid. "Well then?" she asked. Light and friendly, but the tension had returned to her shoulders.

Marcel reached a decision. "You should see this," he said and worked off his left glove. Tandi's eyes widened. Breath hissed between her teeth.

He couldn't blame her. He also winced at the sight of the raised white ridges, outlined with reddish brown that covered his hand from his thumb to the back of his third knuckle. "I always wear a glove lest the sight of it disgust the customers," he said, averting his gaze.

"How'd it happen?" she asked.

"I broke the rules once," he said. He rubbed his scarred fingers together. "Theobromancy can be dangerous. Ever since then, I've been afraid to . . ."

He started as warmth wrapped over his fingers. Her hand, clasping his. "Afraid to break rules?" she asked.

"Yes," he admitted. He looked down, at their entwined hands, her fingers hiding his scars from view. "Maybe Zach won after all," he said. "I trusted the rules to keep me safe, but today, if the fly had been an actual threat . . ."

Maybe he'd tell that to Zach later. It might banish the memory of the sad look he'd given, just before he'd exited. We all have fears, Marcel reflected. *Some are just better at hiding them than others.*

Tandi was silent a moment. Then: "Let's make a promise," she said. "You break a rule occasionally and I'll make sure my no-good trickster of a master, Casey FitzKinley, keeps a few more of his."

He laughed once, softly, and something that had been

bottled up in his chest for too long started to break loose. "I can agree to that," he said.

"Should we seal the deal by going out for coffee?" she asked, smiling.

I really should work on the truffles, he thought. Only one week remaining before the competition, and thanks to Zach's mischief, he was behind. "I'd be honored to go somewhere with you," he found himself saying instead, and Tandi brightened. "Only . . ."

"Yes?" she prompted when he paused.

"Not for coffee, *si vous plait.*"

Tandi burst out laughing. After a moment, Marcel joined in.

The History of a Fruitcake

C. A. ROWLAND

Winner of the 2015 Bethlehem Writers Roundtable Short Story Award

Flour flew as Marlene began whisking it with the macerated fruits and eggs. The pre-baking stage of soaking the fruit had been completed two days ago. Marlene liked to think though, that the first swipe of the whisk was the true beginning of her masterpiece. Mixed together, the cake was just the right blend of fruit and rum, with Marlene's special blend of spices and a secret ingredient. She knew a gift of fruitcake was likely to be ridiculed. At least at first, but her reputation for pies and more traditional cakes extended to the three surrounding counties. Why, she'd been the winner in the best homemade pie contest at the Sanderson County Fair three years running. Her baked goods were much sought after, and she knew once word of her fruitcake got out, there'd be demand for it through the entire holiday season.

Craiseville was a small town of just under ten thousand people. It might seem big to some, but it was the kind of place where everyone knew everyone else's business. Marlene certainly made sure she knew what was going on due to how much she cared about Craiseville. After all, her ancestors had been one of the founding families.

As the fruitcake fermented, Marlene ruminated over who would properly appreciate the gift. She'd make others for her family as her annual contribution to each relative's family gathering. It was a tradition she loved even if it wasn't always valued as much as she thought it should be. For this first one, though, it would be given to someone in her circle of friends. She only had to decide who would most enjoy it. She knew there was a special person who would love it.

Marlene wasn't sure when she first decided she wanted to make the concoction. But she'd dreamed about creating a setting of the graceful flamingos in the front yard as a December scene. A table in the middle would have food, but the star would be a fruitcake. Scarlett had insisted. Of course, she knew Scarlett, the matriarchal pink flamingo, couldn't talk, but she'd learned to trust what she said in dreams. That must have been when she knew she was destined to make a perfect version. Thinking back, Marlene realized she hadn't given her friend Laura a homemade gift in years. While Laura hadn't said she wanted a sweet dessert, Marlene was sure she'd appreciate all the effort in making this particular loaf.

Marlene had changed the Thanksgiving costumes on the birds for more elf-like ones. They were complete with green clothing, bells, and pointy hats, although Marlene hadn't had any red or gold fabric. She'd settled for a plaid left over from St. Patrick's Day but she didn't think anyone would notice. Securing the hats was difficult, so she simply added plaid ties that created a bow under the necks. With fabric to spare, she used the last of the plaid to secure the wrapping paper for the gift.

~~~

Presented with the package, Laura unwrapped the brightly colored paper and forced her mouth into a smile. She rolled the fabric ribbon into a ball, realizing the material was part of Marlene's flamingo family wardrobe. She'd dreaded this year, knowing Marlene always experimented with new recipes
~~~

that she tried out on her friends. With twenty pounds to lose before the holidays, a fruitcake wasn't on her diet. Even if it had been, it was hardly a "treat" she would have asked for. She hated candied anything. Rum made her tongue break out in little blisters to the point she suspected she was allergic. Laura ran her hand through her curly blond hair—a nervous tick she hoped Marlene didn't notice.

"You'll love it," Marlene said. "It's my perfect recipe. Scarlett said so."

Laura stifled an urge to laugh. She wouldn't put fruitcake and perfect in the same sentence. And a flamingo who talked? It was all she could do not to roll her eyes as she said, "I'm sure we'll enjoy it. This was so thoughtful of you."

Laura knew it was the thought that counted, but she also knew her family wouldn't come within two feet of the cake. She resisted the urge to say so. She was loath to throw it away. Marlene and she were friendly, but Marlene was also the town gossip. What if someone saw it in the trash? No, it would be better to pass it on. But what to do with it? Was this something that could be re-gifted? She realized if she didn't want it, no one else might either. Still, there must be someone she could give this to that was appropriate.

Prim and proper, with her straight auburn hair in a classic bun, Dorinda, wasn't the obvious choice for the fruitcake. She straightened her shoulders and drew in a breath, exactly as she always did when facing a judge. The whole town knew she had her eye on the county commissioner position. She'd need all the votes she could get and couldn't afford to appear offended, which Laura knew.

"I wanted to put any bad feelings behind us," Laura said as

she delivered the re-wrapped gift with a plaid bow.

Dorinda had represented the buyer of a piece of land Laura and her husband, Doug, were selling. The negotiations had been long and tedious. If it weren't for the fact her husband's brother was Dorinda's partner, Laura wouldn't have considered giving her anything. But family was family, and it didn't hurt to know someone in power if Dorinda was elected.

Dorinda hated to think about the meaning and motives behind the gift and certainly had no intention of eating the lump of doughy fruit in front of her. The real question was how many times this cake had been re-gifted. She knew Laura didn't bake. She also knew Laura was friends with Marlene. Marlene had cornered Dorinda at a local charity event and bent her ear about publishing a cookbook featuring her family history and her award winning recipes.

"Picture this," Marlene had said. We could include pictures of my flamingos for different holidays throughout."

Dorinda had conceded it was an interesting idea but secretly doubted anyone would buy that type of book.

Dorinda decided her secretary, Debbie, was a safe bet for the gift. She'd add a gift certificate and a few other personal objects, so the fruitcake wasn't the main item. The last thing she wanted was for Debbie to feel slighted. A perfect solution.

Debbie looked at the fruitcake, crossed her arms and wondered if Dorinda had lost her mind. Who gave a fruitcake these days? Or any other time? Must have been a re-gifting. The fabric ribbon was a bit frayed—almost as if it had been tied before or used for something else. And plaid wasn't exactly a holiday fabric. She could have sworn she'd seen that fabric somewhere recently.

It wasn't as if Dorinda was a baker or cook. She was too busy in court and working long hours at the office. Eating it was out of the question. She was diabetic. That fact wasn't common knowledge, and she'd never talked to Dorinda about it. Still, she hated to waste food with so many starving people in the world.

Debbie wondered who had made the cake. Had to be Marlene. She was the only one in town who would think that was a good idea. Normally Debbie loved hearing what she had made and who had received it. She never dreamed she would be included. But no matter, she'd simply pass it on.

At the nursing home, the head nurse, Brenda, removed the fruitcake sitting on the table in front of Debbie's Aunt Judith. The nurse had promised to serve it to the residents, but most of their diets wouldn't allow for it. Since it was likely soaked in alcohol, she wasn't inclined to feed it to them anyway. Instead, she knew her son, Jake, liked sweets. She'd save it for him, just like she did with some of the "treats" Marlene brought the residents. Brenda wasn't sure about some of the concoctions- -strange cakes that included ingredients like sweet potatoes, lavender, Mountain Dew, and green tea. All seemed to be inspired by someone named Scarlett who Marlene talked about. Brenda knew her heart was in the right place, but she just never seemed to consider the residents' restrictive diets. She wondered if the fruitcake was Marlene's. It didn't matter. The residents wouldn't ever know Brenda had not shared it with them. The ones who might, mostly likely wouldn't remember it had ever been there.

When Jake deposited the gift from his mom on the table, Hannah stared for a moment before asking,

"What is that?"

"A fruitcake. Didn't you ever have one for the holidays?"

"I thought they were an urban legend. I've never actually seen one. What are we supposed to do with it?" Hannah asked.

Jake laughed. "Eat it, silly."

"Maybe you will but I'll pass."

"I can't throw it out. One, it's from my mom and two, I'm a chef. We don't throw out perfectly good food."

Hannah's arched eyebrows gave voice to her question of whether the cake was really food, much less in the good category.

Jake and Hannah walked around the fruitcake for a few days. On Thursday evening, they watched an episode of *Top Chef.*

"That's it," he said jumping up.

Hannah stared at him. "What's it?"

"I know what to do with the fruitcake," Jake said as he paced the room.

The Jackson Inn had the only white tablecloth restaurant in Craiseville. Every year, the local book club reserved the private room for their holiday luncheon. In the past years, they had approved the menu in advance but now they allowed the chef to choose for them. This year they were all reading several historical novels set in Rome and requested something suitable in the same theme.

Roast tuna was accompanied by Columella Salad, which their hostess assured them were each prepared in the culinary customs of ancient Rome. Jake brought the desserts in himself as he had the prior year. Each creation rested along the center of an oblong white china plate.

"I know this is not something you expected, but I hope you enjoy it. I've created a deconstructed fruit cake with a vanilla rum crème. The nuts have been caramelized, and the candied fruits serve as the garnish."ww

The ladies looked at each other and tentatively took their first bites. Shoulders relaxed. Conversation returned as the ladies lingered over the dessert. Even some of the foodies among them smiled as they waited for the presidentthe ultimate foodie in the group.

President Marlene took a bite. She had an excellent palate,

and she noted all the ingredients were the same as her recipe. Wondering where Jake's recipe came from, she took a second and third bite. This cake was yummy and certainly an inventive concoction. She knew her food and history. Fruitcake had begun in Rome.

"Very pleasing. And an appropriate dessert for the Roman inspired meal," she said to no one in particular.

Marlene would have to keep her eye on Jake. The fruitcake was quite good, and if his other baked goods were at the same level, she might have a real competitor for the Sanderson County Fair events. The plating was excellent, but the centerpiece on the main table caught her eye—a very nice fabric ribbon bow of green and red plaid. She wasn't sure that was strictly Roman but thought she might take it home with her. The bow could top the holiday tree for the flamingos.

She took another bite and savored the flavors melting in her mouth. The fruitcake was quite tasty, she thought, but the blend of spices was not quite right—it needed her secret ingredient. Otherwise, it would have been perfect.

Bacon

HEADLEY HAUSER

I suppose you might think it's just practical, but it amazes me that I've never seen unsliced bacon—no bacon steaks, no bacon roasts, no bacon fingers or croquets. How is it in a world which calls two almost completely unrelated foods "clam chowder," do we have uniformity on the issue of preparing pork belly? We live in a country in which people that voted for Pat Robertson are living next door to people who voted for Jerry Brown, and we consider "thick slice" a radical departure in the area of breakfast meat.

It's not as if we lack the imagination. I was surprised when someone told me about scallops. What they serve you in a restaurant is rarely a true scallop. Someone just takes some common white fish and cuts it down to little button shapes. (I had always wondered how the little guys swam around.) Why no such innovation with bacon? Oh, I hear you! "Bacon bits!" you say. But bacon bits are just slices crumbled up. If you don't believe me, spend a night at a salad bar matching them up like a jigsaw puzzle. (It's more fun than it sounds and a great conversation starter.)

Could it be that there is something THEY'RE not telling

us? (I've always loved the "they" concept. Isn't it exciting that there might be a people sufficiently motivated to pull themselves away from *Baywatch* re-runs to create dubious conspiracies of minutia and mind control?) Maybe things just aren't the way we think they are at the slaughterhouse.

They say that pigs are highly intelligent. I'll admit that I've not been exposed to pigs a great deal. There wasn't much of an opportunity to see pigs in the neighborhood I was raised (unless you believe what Mrs. Harris said about her ex-husband) but from what little I've observed, I've seen no sign of brilliance among these illuminati of the barnyard. I'll buy that dolphins are smart, living in the sea, swallowing shrimp at will, befriending mermaids, and bopping sharks on the nose. I can believe that chimpanzees are savvy, making neat tree houses, eating high fiber fruits and leaves, staying out of reach of lions and making fun of Tarzan, but what do we see of the pig? Does sleeping in mud and eating excessive amounts of garbage to raise cholesterol and fat content sufficient to invite slaughter sound like an enlightened lifestyle choice?

This is where THEY come in!

THEY don't want you to know, but I've figured it all out. Historians, politicians, zoologists, practitioners of animal husbandry (yes, I laugh when I hear that, too) and several grocers have successfully (for the most part) hidden the fact that at one time, the pig competed with humankind for mastery of the planet.

At that time, pigs were a slim, clean, warrior species. They wrote poetry and dressed in tasteful linen robes and open-toed sandals. Their prowess with the multi-blade sword was admired, feared, and copied. For centuries, the issue was in doubt. The pig armies would march out for honorable combat as we humans sneaked around behind them, toilet papered their rock gardens and painted rude mustaches on their sculptures. We might be speaking grunt today if it weren't for the swine traitor Poq Ye Pyhigue who revealed to us the secret word of pig submission: Soooooouuwwweeeeee! What, you think a simple word could never have such power? C'mon, what did you think the movie Babe was *really* about?

A once mighty people now lives in squalor, consumes refuse, and follows calmly on that last long mile to their extermination. Their only hope, that high cholesterol may take a few of us with them. Reaching the abattoir, they are allowed to hold for the only time in their lives the weapon of their people, the multi-blade sword. In a tradition since copied by the samurai class in Japan, the noble pig commits hari-kari leaving his belly in several long even strips.

Perhaps it's better that people not know the truth. Our breakfast plates are salty enough, without tears of remorse, regret, and recrimination. We dare not attempt liberation. The backlash would once again threaten our very existence. There's an entire wing of the Pentagon dedicated to contingencies in case pigs someday develop immunity to the farmer's call.

Like a red and white flag of defiance, the bacon strip waves and curls at the bottom of my skillet. No steak, roast or kabob could express so well, no scallop could define in such certain terms, the dignity and tragedy that is the porcine karma.

Hey, what would you call a bacon scallop? Would you want to eat a pig belly button?

Our Town is Different

SALLY PARADYSZ

Clark swiveled on her diner counter stool just as a man pushed through the swinging door of the kitchen. Massive of girth, with a jet-black mustache, he headed her way. Stopping beside her, he met her eyes and spoke quietly.

"Bev says you want a cooking job?"

Clark straightened. She had said "chef position." She opened her mouth to reply, but he held up his hand.

"Sorry, hon, but I can't hire you."

Clark looked at her hands, then up at him, "But I'm a terrific cook. I only need a chance. I'll work for free today—well, just for a meal maybe—and you can see . . ." She hated to beg, but knew she was.

"I wish I could, but I got all the help I need."

Clark looked over and saw a frail-looking old man at a nearby table watching with half a smile. She felt her cheeks redden.

"Look," she said, leaning toward the diner owner and whispering so as not to be heard by the nosy old-timer. "I've nowhere to go. I need work. You won't be sorry if you hire me."

"Maybe, but I still can't hire you." He shook his head like

he really regretted it, then moved to the cash register when a customer walked up to pay his bill. Clark stared, first at him, then at the wall behind him that was covered in cardboard signs listing the "Specialties of the House." Lobster roll (market price). Fried onion rings. Fish and chips. Clam chowdah. *Cute.* Ice cream with jimmies. Nothing that special. She could have people lined up around the block to eat at this greasy spoon if they'd only give her a chance.

"Hey," the big man said, returning to her spot at the counter. "If you need work, you might ask that guy over there." He pointed in the direction of the old man. "I heard him saying he needs someone to cook, do some light cleaning."

She looked over. "I'm not interested in keeping house for some old geezer. I'm a chef."

He shrugged. "Well, anyway, here's some money to tide you over. It's not much, but it's all I can handle right now." He held out a ten.

Clark looked from his face to the bill, and back to the wall.

"I don't take charity," she snarled and spun her stool away from the massive man.

"Suit yourself." He sauntered back to the kitchen.

Clark stood and grabbed her purse and duffel bag and rushed out the door. She didn't get far. Her knees were wobbly, so she scurried to the side of the diner, sat on the pavement, and leaned on the dumpster. "What now?" she mumbled. "What now?"

Eyes closed, legs akimbo, Clark rested her head against the warmth of the sun-drenched metal. Tears slipped down her face, and she brushed them away with the back of her hand. She no longer cared about the new white shirt she bought with the last of her money. It didn't matter anymore. It just didn't matter.

Clark thought this town might be different. It felt different when she got off the bus that morning. Locals greeted each other as they passed in the street. Some even said "hi" to her. The town green had lush grass, flowering trees, and planters filled with flowers. Kids played tag among monuments and a bandstand. She didn't remember ever being that carefree.

After an hour she stood, brushed the dirt from her behind, and turned toward the bus station. If she wasn't going to earn food, she might get lucky and find an abandoned lunch on one of the long wooden seats.

No such luck today. *A podunk town in Nowhere, New Hampshire. I should have known better*, she thought. She rummaged in her duffel bag. Nothing to eat there. The last crumbs were breakfast. She hoped she'd have a job by lunch.

She slumped on a bench that was out of sight of the ticket window. Again she closed her eyes. She was even more tired than hungry.

Someone was shaking her awake. "What? What?" Clark said angrily, trying to gain some composure. She looked up and saw an old man still with his hands on her shoulder. She batted and kicked him away.

"What? Do I have your bench or something?" She thrust her hand into her bag. She had a chef's knife just inside the fold. She'd sewn it there last week after being attacked by a homeless man in a station just like this. The guy stood there with half a smile.

"Wait," she said with disgust. "You're that geezer from the diner. What do you want?"

"I've an offer for ya if you come with me," the old man said, gesturing back toward the entrance.

"I'm not going anywhere with you, creep. Go home to your wife."

He shuffled back. "I don't have a wife. I do have a farm, and I do have a friend who lives with me. I need someone to cook and clean, do laundry and other things around the house, and help me with the barn chores and our horses."

"I'm not a hired hand. I'm a chef." She jutted out her chin.

"Oh, for the love of Mike. Stop with the cooking stuff. You need a job, and I need help. You want it or not?"

"No!"

"Okay then, but if you change your mind, my farm's the last big one on the main road heading west out of town. Fences need paint. You can't miss it. Name's Howie Sharpe. Glad to meet ya."

Howie walked out through the door of the bus station and disappeared. Moments later, an engine coughed. She saw an old truck pull away. Clark knew it was his. It had to be. *It's as old as he is*, she thought. *How lucky, an old geezer with an ancient truck wants to hire me. Put me to work doing laundry, cleaning, and cooking. I guess he thinks I'm desperate.*

"Oh, God," she said aloud, lying back down on the bench. "I am."

She turned her head and saw a couple of unopened energy bars and a bottle of water on the bench across from her. She scrambled over and snatched them up. She ate the bars quickly before whoever left them came back for them, and stowed the bottled water in her duffel.

Clark stayed in the bus station all afternoon, but knew she couldn't linger all night. Her back hurt, and her knees ached. She had to go, but where? She wondered if that old guy even had a farm. Where did he say it was? The west side of town?

She kept up a good pace, walking on the main road toward the sunset. After dusk, she spied a rusty mailbox with the names W. Baker and H. Sharpe printed on the side. The lid was open, and it leaned hard to the left, right in front of a fence that desperately needed a coat of paint. Down the long dirt drive-way, she spotted the farmhouse. There was a light burning in a downstairs window.

When she reached the front steps, she looked up and was startled to see Howie sitting in a rocker on the porch.

"Took you long enough to make up your mind."

Clark looked at her feet. "Okay, old geezer, you were right. I'm desperate. Do you have a place for me to sleep tonight or what?" She looked around, not sure she could trust the guy. "The barn is good. Tomorrow morning I'll make you breakfast and then be on my way."

Howie nodded. "The barn is just over there. Go down the aisle between the stalls and there's a door to the right. It's the tack room. Blankets and a cot are in there. Help yourself to the peanut butter and bread in the small fridge. See you in the morning."

Clark woke early the next day. *Too early*, she thought, trying to work the soreness out of her muscles from the long hike the night before. She'd nearly finished off the bread and peanut butter, and was glad she had the bottle of water. She thought about just ditching the geezer and hitting the road, but decided to keep her end of the bargain and make breakfast for what's his name, Howie. She wondered about W. Baker. Howie said he lived with a friend. Was it a woman? She hoped it wasn't another creep. She picked up her blankets, folded them and put them back on the shelf above the cot. Leaving her purse and duffel on the bed, Clark walked into the aisle and stared at the two horses--one short and one tall. The tall one had his neck stretched over the half-door of its stall. The pony trotted around its enclosure. She inhaled the aroma of hay, corn, molasses, and the unmistakable scent of manure. *Funny*, she thought. *It actually smells kind of good.*

The horses watched her as she skirted past them. The pony gave a soft whinny. They big one was huge, and a little scary, but at least they both seemed friendly.

The farmhouse, like the fence in front of it, needed paint, but all in all it looked sturdy. *Better than the hunk of metal junk of a trailer where I grew up.* She knocked on a side door that looked well used, then opened it to find herself in a huge eat-in kitchen. Howie sat at a table drinking coffee.

"Come on in, uh . . ." he said. "What's your name? I can't go around calling you girlie all morning."

"My name is Clarkson Channing. Call me Clark."

"Sounds like a man's name to me, but Clark it is."

"I said I'd make you breakfast and I will. May I have a cup of coffee with you first, uhhh Howie?"

"Nope, I'm out to the barn. Need to feed the horses. You

can find your way around the kitchen, right? Food pantry's over there by the stove. Weezer is out doing his chores; we'll both be back in an hour. That's how long you have to fix us something to eat." With a chuckle, he walked out the door.

Weezer? What kind of name was that?

Clark went to the fridge and peeked in. She pulled out egg cartons, slices of thick ham, cheese, butter, and cream. Flour, sugar, and tea canisters sat side by side on the scratched counters. *Hope they're full.* She opened the pantry door; it looked well stocked for someone who didn't want to cook for himself. She grabbed a few items and brought them all to the counter. Between drinking coffee from a chipped mug, and eating three pieces of toast, Clark set about her task.

Exactly an hour later, Howie walked in with the shortest man she'd ever seen. "This is my friend, Weezer Baker. There aren't many little people around these parts, but we've known and respected each other for a very long time."

"Happy to know you, Weezer," Clark said staring at him. Remembering herself, she extended her hand.

Weezer nodded and gave her hand a quick tug. He looked gentle, but his eyes were a fierce blue. For some unknown reason, she felt safe in his presence.

"Smells good in here," Howie said. "C'mon, Weezer. We gotta go wash up before we can dig into this breakfast she's made us." The two men left the kitchen and headed toward the back of the house.

While they were out of the room, Clark opened the oven and removed what she had prepared. She set fresh fruit and juice in the middle of the table alongside a small glass of flowers she'd picked from those growing beside the back door.

When the men walked in, she had set two places and was in the process of making a fresh pot of coffee. Her stomach rumbled, and she tried to cover the noise by clearing her throat. She turned and saw the old guys just standing there.

"So, this is breakfast," Clark said.

They men sat and held their hands in their laps.

"What's wrong?" Clark asked feeling a bit anxious.

Weezer finally found his voice. "Nothing's wrong. This looks like three meals in one. Where did you find all this food?"

She looked at the array. Six Eggs Benedict made with ham rather than Canadian bacon, covered with homemade Hollandaise sauce; a Florentine omelet; two apple crepes with a warm apple-cinnamon compote, topped with vanilla-scented whipped cream; cornbread; and a mountain of shredded and lightly sautéed garlic and herb potatoes.

"I made it from the ingredients you had on hand. Hope you like it. After all your hard work, you must be starving."

Howie looked at Weezer; Weezer looked at Howie. "Clark, you are amazing." Howie slammed a hand on the table and chuckled. "I knew it. I just knew it. When you told Mac you were a great cook at the diner yesterday, I figured you had more going for you than you looked like you did. Appearances can be deceiving." He winked at Weezer, who nodded. "Where in the living hell did you learn to cook like this?"

"I used to wash dishes at a fancy restaurant in Lowell. I kept my head down and my ears open and watched each and every dish that left the kitchen. At night when the chefs left, I read their recipes and looked at the ingredients in their coolers. Sometimes I hid in the back, and when everyone left, I'd light a couple of candles and try to imitate what they made that day. After a year or so, I began to have a feeling for what went together, cheeses or sauces or wine combinations. I loved cooking." She couldn't help but smile at the memory.

Weezer leaned forward. "So what happened?"

Howie slapped Weezer's arm. "You don't have to tell us unless you want, girlie."

"That's okay." Clark turned back to the counter. "One night a chef came back for his set of knives he'd left behind and caught me red handed. Kicked me out and that was the end of my kitchen career."

"Oh, that's rough," Howie said. Clark scowled and turned to see if he was mocking her, but his expression was sympathetic.

Weezer chimed in. "Thanks for sharing that, Clark." He picked up a fork. "But, I've never seen anything like this made up in an hour. Good God, girl. Let's eat!"

There was not much conversation going on for the next few minutes until Howie looked up from his plate.

"Clark, you're not eating. What's the matter?"

"I didn't know if it was okay for me to eat with you."

"Well, why not? I asked you to come here and cook. That means you eat, too. I've never had food like this before, Clark. You have a gift here, something valuable to hold on to."

"Thanks, Geezer," Clark said, then put her hand over her mouth. "Ooops. Sorry."

Weezer winked at her and Howie laughed. "You know, I'd try to stop you from using that word, but I'm afraid you'd run away," Howie said with his mouth half-full.

"I won't run. . . . Actually, I was wondering if you'd let me stay here for a few days until I get back on my feet. I used all my money buying new clothes to try to get a job." She looked down at her by-now dirty jeans. "Since Lowell, I've been going from town to town, hoping that someone would hire me on. I did anything to earn a little money, but I never accepted favors or worked in a sleazy place."

"Good for you," Weezer said.

"Do you think it's possible for me to stay in the barn?" She realized she had let down her guard. It was usually her constant companion. What was wrong with her? She didn't even know these men. But something about them . . .

Howie sat back in his chair with his hands crossed over his stomach. "You are like a bright light in this farmhouse. I'd like for you to stay."

"I'd like to give you a chance, too," Weezer said. "If you're honest with us and keep your head on your shoulders, you are welcome to stay. Let's see how it works out for all of us." He rubbed his stubbly cheek.

"I gotta confess," Howie said, "it's not like we know nothing about you. I took a look in your duffel to see if you had a gun or drugs, or were something different than we thought, but I found nothing other than that knife. And it looked like a cook's knife, so I figure that's why you got it."

"Hey! That bag is my personal stuff. Keep out of it." Clark said.

"Calm down," Howie said. "I was just taking precautions."

Clark looked at the table. "I guess that makes sense," she said.

Weezer asked, "Where'd you grow up?"

He's nice, Clark thought, *but now I'm not so sure about Howie. I hope I can trust him.* "I grew up down by the South Shore. Brockton."

"Really? I spent some time there, too," Weezer said.

"My dad died shortly after I was born and my mom drank," Clark said, sitting down and filling her plate. "We lived in a tiny, run-down trailer until my mom walked away one day."

"Then what happened?" Howie asked. Weezer swatted *his* arm.

"You know what? I think I've said enough for one day."

"Yeah. We gotta get back to work anyhow," Weezer said, hopping down from his chair.

After the men left the house, Clark cleaned up the breakfast dishes and then walked out to the barn. She approached the pony's stall but stayed more than an arm's length away. The animal's nose looked soft, and its eyes were a beautiful deep brown. She wanted to reach out but dashed into the tack room instead.

With the door closed, Clark felt safe. Carefully, she laid down on the cot, stuffing the pillow behind her head. A real bed, not a bus station bench. All hers, at least for now.

Two hours later Howie woke her by knocking loudly on the door. "Hey Clark, it's time for lunch. What about your side of the bargain?"

"Oh man," Clark said rubbing her face with her hands. "I fell asleep. I'll be right there."

After sandwiches of sausages, onions and peppers, and hot rolls, Howie suggested she go back to her room and rest some more. "You been on the road a while. We won't bother you. We just need dinner about six. You can catch up on the laundry and stuff beginning tomorrow. Just consider this a rest day."

Back on her cot in the tack room, Clark's eyes closed, and she thought about her mom. She still missed her. *Maybe I'll be able to find her one day, and give her something to be proud of.* She opened her eyes but closed them again. Slowly.

Clark woke and stretched. She felt more rested than she had in—well she didn't know how long. She exited the tack room and loped toward the house. When she got to the kitchen, she checked the clock. Six-thirty already. Dinner was late.

"Hello? Howie? Weezer? I'm so sorry. I'll get dinner started right away." She turned toward the living room when no one answered, and saw Weezer on the floor, cradling Howie's head in his lap. Weezer looked up at Clark, then back down at Howie. "He fell, Clark," Weezer said. I don't know if he tripped or had a heart attack or something, but he's unconscious. I called nine-one-one. The ambulance will be here any minute."

"Oh, Weezer. I should have been here."

He shook his head. "You're here now. Grab some blankets, and a wet cloth for his head."

"Okay." She returned moments later. "Gosh. There's blood on the floor."

"We'll clean it later."

It was a heart attack. The doctors considered surgery but told Howie it was too risky. Howie said he understood. He'd lived a good long life and was willing to leave it up to God to decide when it was his time. But he wanted to do that in his own bed.

They brought Howie home, but he was too weak to leave his room. Clark finished all her chores each day and then kept Howie company. Friends dropped by to visit. Some left flowers.

A couple of men helped Weezer out with Howie's chores. One woman named Amelia brought some food by one day just as Clark and Weezer were about to sit down to dinner. Amelia joined them for one of Clark's better creations. She was proud of the meal, but Weezer embarrassed her by how he praised her cooking to their friend.

Clark could see Howie was getting weaker every day and was angry that there was nothing the doctors could do to stop it. Only four weeks after his fall, Howie died. Both Weezer and Clark were by his side.

After the funeral, Clark and Weezer scattered Howie's ashes on the grassy knoll by the pond, just like he wanted.

Several weeks later, Weezer said, "Howie only knew you for a short time, but he liked you. I think you made his last days some of his happiest. Thank you for that."

Clark sat down next to Weezer. "Where did you meet Howie?" she asked.

"He had sixty acres left to him when his parents died in a car accident. His land and mine were connected. We used to eat breakfast at the diner together there once a week. Then, once in a while, when we had a little extra, we'd treat ourselves to a trip to Amelia's Café. You met Amelia. She's the one that brought the food over that day. She has a fancy place in town. I'll take you there someday."

Clark raised her eyebrows. She didn't know they ever had a "little extra."

"The first winter after the accident," Weezer continued, "I found Howie snuggled into the back of that old truck, trying to stay warm. There're no buildings on his tract—just field, so he had no place to stay. He was a pretty decent mechanic—had to be to keep that old truck running—but he was having trouble with his health. He was always kind of fragile, you know. He couldn't keep a job because of it. I think that's why he wanted to give you a chance. He knew what it was like to need help."

"That's so sad."

"He didn't want to take charity, so I let him stay in the tack room, just like you. When it turned to real frigid weather, I asked him to come into the house. He said the only way he'd stay was if we considered our two properties one large farm. I said that worked for me and over the years we left our assets to each other in our wills."

"Was it an even trade?"

"Yep. He grew beautiful Timothy hay and oats for the horse farms around the area. And I had ten rocky acres and an old farmhouse. Even trade."

Clark felt heartsick for Weezer.

"Well, Clark," Weezer said, "it's you and me now. You can leave if you want; it's up to you. Don't stay on my account because I'll be okay. But I'd like you to stay." He turned his head and swiped at his eyes with his sleeve. "It's just damn sad. So damn sad."

"I can stay, Weezer," she said, reaching out to touch his hand. "I have no other place to go. If it's okay with you, I'd still like to see if I can find a restaurant to hire me on so I can pay my way."

"If you cook for me, do laundry, and help me care for the horses, I'll never charge you a penny for living here, but I can't offer a paycheck. I still need the help. I know my age and the condition of my health, and neither is in my favor. Little people have different health problems. Howie did what he could in his fragile body, but he tired easily as he aged. Guess we all do."

"It's a deal. Let's make some tea and toast now in the kitchen." Clark said softly. "Both of us need to eat a little something and then rest."

After the kettle boiled, they sat at the kitchen table across from each other.

"Tell me a bit about your mother," Weezer said, taking a sip from his mug.

"She tried hard to be a good mother." Clark closed her eyes and inhaled the herbal scent. "When she was sober, she was gentle and loving. Mom always said I was the light of her life, but when things got too heavy, she walked away."

"Why? Were you a burden to your mom as you got older?"

Clark creased her forehead. "I hope not." She took a sip. "When I was twelve, I kinda came to a crossroads. Mom said that I needed to walk a steady road because she wasn't able to do that, and she knew where that could lead."

Weezer cleared his throat. "That was rough to hear, I imagine."

"Yep. Mom said everyone's life has that kind of moment. A moment when things can go either way, up or down, right or wrong. One has to decide for themselves. I guess that's why she walked away—to give me a chance at a stable life."

Weeks passed calmly for Clark, but as it did, she became more certain that Weezer needed her there. Keeping the farm going drained him. She cooked and baked everything he loved best, but it was hard work with everything else she was doing. Still, she finally had a place to call home, and that was special. And every once in a while, when they had a little extra, Weezer would take her to Amelia's Café. It was just the kind of place Clark hoped to work someday.

One afternoon after lunch, Weezer turned to her and said, "Let's talk."

"Sure. What's on your mind?"

"It's all about love, girlie. Believing and trusting that we are where we're supposed to be. I think that's why you're here. Why you found your way to this small town and us."

"You think so?"

"Yes. This village has something very important, something that has been here forever." He looked at her sideways. "Maybe you've noticed?"

Clark wasn't sure what he meant but kept quiet, hoping he'd go on.

"Again it's about caring for one another as friends and neighbors. Other communities around here have lost it—or never had it. Each town looks like the others. Too big, too impersonal. But ours is different. It's always been different. I've worked hard all my life to keep it that way. I love this rural community. Of course, sometimes I hate it, too." There was a twinkle in his eye.

"Really?"

"Yup. You know what I hate about it? Everybody knows everybody else here and always has. You know what I love about it? Everybody knows everybody else here and always has."

Clark chuckled. "Well, I can't imagine that. I've never stayed in one place long enough, but maybe now I can, Weezer. I love it here. I love the horses and, and, and, I love you." She sprang to her feet and gave him a hug.

"I love you, too, girlie," he said, patting her shoulders. When she'd returned to her seat, he said, "Tell me. What happened after your mother walked away when you were twelve?"

"Well, after the police discovered I was there alone, they made me a ward of the state. I went to a lot of foster homes. Some decent, some marginal, and one that was downright frightening. At sixteen I left there, knowing that my life was in more danger in that home than it was on the road. I've been traveling and supporting myself for four years." She paused. "Sometimes better than others. This place is the best I've ever found. I never want to leave."

"It's settled then. You're here to stay. Oh, and you need to move into the house," Weezer said, standing up. "Pick one of the bedrooms and make it yours. Fix it up your way."

"I will, and thank you." It was then that Clark realized just how much Weezer had to give. His intelligence and compassion were beyond what she imagined.

~~~

Weezer took over all the chores and Clark helped the best she could. Neighbors dropped by. Someone painted the fence out front just before Thanksgiving. They invited friends over to share the holiday, and Clark cooked for all of them—even Amelia.
~~~

In December, Weezer brought home a Christmas tree, and they decorated it together. It was the first real tree Clark had had in years. His gift to Clark was a set of knives. Professional knives.

"How did you know?" Clark said, tears in her eyes.

"Amelia from the restaurant told me every chef has her own knives and never lets anybody else use them. Ever." He rubbed his brow with his thumb. "Now these are yours."

With her new tools, Clark experimented, designing recipes on her own, hoping that one day she could write a cookbook, or maybe become a sous-chef in a nice restaurant. She spent hours each day researching, making changes according to taste.

Weezer loved every meal she made. Her skills were getting stronger, and she knew it. Her hands began to look like a chef's, red and with small cuts all over them. She wasn't earning money, but she had no bills. What she had was a place to live, but she wanted to get good enough to ask Amelia for a job. She knew she had a lot to learn and far to go, but she was taking great pains to get there.

Weezer taught her how to ride, and soon she was able to take off every late afternoon and ride to the edges of the farm and up into the hills. She loved that part of every day. The time when the sun would begin to set, painting the farm with colors of gold, crimson, and finally indigo. It was as if nature was giving her permission to enjoy herself after a hard day of work.

⁓

"Clarkson!" Weezer shouted from the living room a few months later.

"What?" she yelled back. "I'm busy making the anniversary dinner to commemorate Howie's death and the love we have for him." She noticed he used her full name. He never did that.

"Come. Come quickly."

Clark set her bowl down, shut off the stove, and went into the living room. Weezer was resting in his favorite lounge chair.

"So what is it, mister? Do you want this extraordinary

dinner or not this evening?" she said in a teasing voice.

Weezer didn't answer. She looked at him more closely and realized he was not responsive. At all. Clark ran to the phone and punched in 911. Last time it was Weezer who had made the call. She wouldn't stay on the line as they asked because she needed to get back to Weezer. She didn't want anyone listening in on what could be her last bit of time with him.

"Oh Weezer," Clark said softly while she leaned in close. "Don't leave me, please. You're the only family I have right now. Don't go yet. I don't know how to manage the farm. I love you, Weezer, please don't go. Please."

～

Time passed. Again. Not so quickly, though. Clark felt sad a good part of the time. She had scattered Weezer's ashes alongside Howie's and felt confident that the two of them were still watching over her.

A month after the funeral, Weezer's lawyer called Clark. "Can you come over and pick up a letter Weezer left for you with his will?"

"Today?"

"Sooner the better. I'll leave it with the secretary."

"What is . . ." The line went dead.

By the time Clark got back from the lawyer's office, it was late afternoon. She stuck the letter between her back and the waist of her jeans and tacked up the bigger horse. When she got to the pond, she dismounted and tied him to the nearby tree.

"Okay guys, I have the letter," Clark said sitting down where their ashes had become part of the soil. "I'm reading it now." Moments later she stood. "No! Weezer. What have you given me?"

The farm was Clark's. The deed in the envelope gave proof.

She couldn't believe it, but after an hour she got on her horse. She rode into the hills as she always had, but it was different this time as she looked down upon the farm. There it sat in late afternoon shadows. All hers.

"I'm so proud of it," she said, leaning on her horse's neck. "So proud."

~

In mid-spring, she leased Howie's part of the farm for the summer months. A neighboring farmer would work the sixty acres, raising Timothy and oats for local horse farms. She kept the ten acres that were Weezer's, and proudly took care of them, working to exhaustion and beyond every day, and exercising the horse and pony in the hours before dusk.

Weezer left her enough money to manage it all nicely—money he'd earned over all those years of farming and saving.

A few weeks later, Amelia called. It was late to receive calls, but Clark answered anyway. "Clark?" Amelia asked.

"Yes."

"This is Amelia from the Café. How are you doing, dear? Everything okay at the farm?"

"I'm making do. Thanks for asking."

"I don't know how you'll feel about it, but I'd like to make you an offer."

Does she want to buy the farm? Clark wondered.

"I'd like you to consider a position as a sous-chef here at the Café."

Clark wasn't sure she understood clearly. "You're offering me a job in your restaurant?"

"Yes. You're a terrific cook, but a little untrained. I think we can help each other out. We need a sous-chef, and you need a mentor. What do you say?"

"Well, thank you. I'm honored. You won't be disappointed. I'll work very hard for you."

With the income from her job, Clark hired a part-time handyman to look after the horses and the farm.

After six months, Clark had learned more than in all her time as a dishwasher and cook for Howie and Weezer—not just about cooking, but about running a restaurant. It was even better than she imagined.

One day, Amelia took Clark aside. "It's time for me to take my old bones away from New Hampshire winters," she said, a gleam in her eye.

"Oh no, are you closing for the season?" Clark worried that her dream had come to an end.

"No. I'm leaving the place in capable hands."

Clark wondered who her new boss would be. "Whose hands?" she asked.

"Yours."

Clark didn't breathe.

"On one condition," Amelia said, holding up a finger. "You have to run it like I've showed you. Pay every employee first, and then tend to the other expenses. We take care of each other here."

Weezer was right, Clark thought. *Focusing on friends and neighbors was what separated this town from others.*

"And when I come back in the spring," Amelia continued, "if all goes well, we'll be partners."

Clark vowed to Howie and Weezer each time she rode by the pond that she was doing her part to keep their town special. She promised them that the farm would live on in love and caring as it always had. And if Amelia needed a place to live or to be cared for in her older years, there was room in the farmhouse for her, too.

"Hey, old geezers," Clark said from her horse one late summer day. "You remember that guy I hired on part time? He says he needs to look for a full-time job." Clark laughed. "I think he's capable of working the Timothy fields along with doing the barn chores. What do you think about my keeping up the town tradition by helping him out, too?"

Cake

E. L. RYAN

Ada shivered in her thin, chic coat and fiddled with the temperamental lock. A mountain of legal paperwork lay heaped on her desk, and her phone chimed with another text. The overcast morning beckoned her to nap, but she clutched her steaming coffee and dug into her work.

Several hours and license agreements later, Ada yawned and stretched back in the creaking chair. The law offices hummed with chattering paralegals and murmuring clients.

A tap of high heels startled Ada, and she pulled a neck muscle. "Mrs. Gupta. I was just . . ."

"Relaxing, I noticed." The senior law partner stood in her pinstripe suit and placed a white container on Ada's desk. "My son's birthday party is this afternoon."

"Congratulations. What's in the box?"

"A gluten-free, wheat-free, sugar-free, hypoallergenic cake." Ada blinked. "Is anything even in there?"

"I would never tolerate my boy eating any high-fructose filth. In any case, the bakery fouled up and delivered it here."

"I see, but how does this involve me?"

"So glad you asked." Gupta produced a scribbled note. "Get

this cake to the rock-climbing gym in Southeast before noon. The nanny shouldn't arrive with the guests until then."

"I'm an attorney, not a courier."

"Today you're both. How special for you."

"How am I supposed to get across town?" Ada glanced at the threatening skies. "And isn't there some kind of festival going on downtown?"

"Isn't there always? But if you can't manage this favor, I'm sure I will remember this at your upcoming performance review." Gupta's lips pressed into a humorless smile. "You know the other partners defer to me on personnel matters."

"Of course." Ada set her jaw. "I'll handle this, Mrs. Gupta."

Ada texted some of her friends in the city and called several cab companies, but none would promise a ride until far too late. A long walking route meandered through rundown neighborhoods and placed her at the gym after lunchtime.

Her smartphone buzzed on the polished oak, and a cheery text from Meghan offered her a glimmer of hope and a pang of apprehension. Ada lifted the surprisingly dense confection by the blue twine and hustled outside towards the rendezvous.

A half dozen picnic tables beside the local tavern stood empty due to the early hour and damp conditions. Grime and bleach wafted from inside the establishment, and the patrons eyed Ada through the dingy windows.

"Hey." Meghan waved, strutting down the block. "There you are."

Ada exhaled and forced a smile. "Thanks for coming."

"Well, I owe you a favor or two." Meghan adjusted a messenger bag over her shoulders. "I've just got to unload some craft whiskey real quick."

"Can't it wait? I have to make this delivery."

"Serving subpoenas?" Meghan sniffed at the cake box. "Tasty treats to entice people to accept the unpalatable papers?"

Ada regarded her college roommate's plunging neckline and said, "Or unpalatable booze."

Meghan missed the implication. "What?"

"Nothing. Sorry, just zero time today."

"Don't worry." Meghan resumed her lopsided grin and withdrew an amber liquor bottle from her bag. "I'll have you to Southeast with time to spare. Come on in with me."

The barflies perked up on the saleswoman's approach, and Ada lingered alone on the sidewalk.

Ada's feet ached in her heels, and she set the cake box on a relatively dry table. Several idle minutes passed before she wedged the loose twine around the corners and eased the flimsy cardboard skywards.

A superhero sculpted from colored frosting posed on the squat pastry before an errant raindrop melted a saccharine hand. Ada yelped and ducked inside the pub to escape the cloudburst.

Dried beer and antiseptic soap on the linoleum tiles forced her to stumble in front of the businessmen, activists, and drunks. Ada managed a nod and eyes dug into her back as she held her nose against the scent of freshly burned grease and hurried past the taps.

Meghan bent over the brass railing and stretched to pluck a few shot glasses behind the bar. She deftly poured the whiskey and extolled the flavorful virtues. The bartender swirled a fresh cocktail, scanning the motley crowd for reactions.

A construction worker smirked at Ada, rubbed his scruffy beard, and reached for the splayed cardboard package. Meghan planted a hand on his chest and pushed him back onto the stool. She slid him a drink and said, "Enjoy this and keep your fingers away from my girl's box."

Onlookers chuckled, and Ada slipped into a booth. Her attempts to repair the frosting only produced smudges, so she gave up and retied the string. Activating her phone, she scowled at the myriad throbbing-red traffic indicators. The rain intensified outside, and Meghan clunked down the half empty bottle beside the cake.

"Figure six shots to get drunk, fourteen shots a bottle, twelve bottles a case, and ten cases." Meghan's genuine smile displayed a prominent, malformed cuspid. "I just made a couple hundred wasted people and rent at the same time."

"Great. Can we go?"

"After the owner finishes the paperwork." She leaned down and whispered, "You know, if we kissed right now, I could probably double the order."

"What?"

"Just saying. I doubt an obsession with haute couture is keeping their eyes glued to my ass. You have to work reality a little."

"Sounds ethical."

"Said the lawyer." Meghan took the opposite bench seat and twanged the cake twine. "This part of your salaried duties?"

"Just a favor." Ada tucked the box into her crossed arms. "I still have some self-respect."

Meghan's distinctive tooth disappeared. "Sure."

～ゝ

The wipers squeaked on the dry windshield as the deluge abated. Meghan wove her whirring electric smart-car through the streets and quipped, "Relax. What is your problem?"

Ada pocketed her phone and cinched her fingers around the crinkling box. "Nothing."

"Really?" Meghan pouted deliberately. "I'm driving for your errand in my company car, but you seem pissed at me."

"Not at you."

"Sure."

Ada sighed. "Between my loans and rent, I cannot lose this job. Which my boss knows all too well. And abuses all too frequently."

"So put a stop to it."

"Stop." Ada pointed at a red light.

"Yeah, that's what I'm . . ."

"Stop!"

A traffic camera flashed, and Meghan slammed on the brakes, launching the cake from Ada's lap. The seatbelt bit into the lawyer as she scrambled for the box. The cake softly squished inside the container, and Ada winced.

"That's a ticket. Damn." Meghan swore as she turned into the gym parking lot.

⌒

Ada jumped out onto the curb and hustled through the puddles. Once inside, she approached the front desk and asked, "Where's the Gupta party?"

A bored attendant tapped a paper sign without looking up. "Closed for a private event."

"I know." The clock on the computer clicked past noon. "This is for the event. A cake."

"Whatever." He lifted his dull eyes. "Back behind the Iceberg at the top of stairs."

Dozens of tall, colored slabs at strange angles filled the spotless rock climbing gym. "Which is . . ."

"Big blue. Left around it, straight ahead, then up."

She navigated the plush safety floor and ascended the painted stairs, rushing past a middle-aged janitor. Built into the side of the cavernous building, an isolated room overlooked the various rock attractions. Tinted windows offered a view of decorations suited for a child's birthday, but no guests.

"Made it." Ada sighed, shoved the door, and bruised herself against the unyielding handle.

"You're a bit early," the janitor said from the staircase with a nervous smile. "Still locked up."

"What?" She gasped for breath.

"A woman called and pushed back the party by an hour."

The man shrugged. "We like to keep the place pristine for the client. Company policy."

"Of course." Ada let her head tilt back towards the smooth sheet metal wall. "Can you unlock it?"

"I'd have to get the manager."

A moment of silence passed before Ada felt compelled to add, "Would you please?"

"Right." The man trundled back down the stairs. "Sure."

Meghan arrived a minute later, sauntering at her casual pace. "Hey. This place looks pretty swanky."

Ada leaned on a painted railing overlooking the belay wall. "I guess."

"All right, come on. Up. No moping." Meghan pulled on Ada's arm, disturbing the box balanced on the railing.

Meghan's mouth hung ajar.

"What?"

The cake tumbled in free fall and landed with a messy splat. The janitor stood near the epicenter with his trousers violently frosted, and Ada slumped against the railing.

"Oh."

～∽

Ada shivered in the artificial chill of the grocery store and complained, "This doesn't seem right."

"Feels fine to me." Meghan scrutinized her reflection in the streaked chrome edge of the refrigerated case. "My second moving violation this month, on the other hand, feels less fine."

"Sorry about that. I'll pay it."

A portly baker hustled out and presented them with a freshly decorated, sugar-infused cake. "How's this?"

"Close enough."

～∽

The Hunt

Carol L. Wright

The hunter crept across the deep-green carpet. His prey dawdled mere yards away, apparently unaware of his approach. He crouched down, eyes trained on the beast, watching for any sign of alarm. Nothing yet, but the hunter's nerves sharpened, alert to any risk of flight. He struggled to quell an involuntary twitch of his upper lip as he slunk forward, careful not to make a sound.

He thought about his circumstances. If he could, he would take a life this day. And without remorse. Why was that old song running through his head? Was it from the movie *Aladdin* that the kids played incessantly when they were young? The line "gotta eat to live; gotta steal to eat." But in this case, he wasn't planning to steal. He would kill if he had the chance.

He wasn't very hungry, but he knew that if he did not take this opportunity it might be many days before he found such easy prey again. By then he could starve. No. He had to strike now and secure a meal while he could, to keep hunger at bay for another day.

Another day.

And what did he have to look forward to in the days to

come? More of the same? Seeking food, clean water, and a safe place to rest. His demands were few, but they were crucial to his survival. He needed to keep his strength up to avoid becoming prey to a larger beast. As age slowed his reflexes, it was more important than ever.

His target froze. Had it become aware of his approach? Crouching lower, the hunter took aim. It was now or never. He had to make his move.

Flinging out his front paws, he pounced. The housefly sped off toward the ceiling and up the staircase. The hunter followed for a few steps, but decided instead to take a bath, turning his humiliation into the appearance of a choice. Besides, his human should be home soon.

There was, after all, more than one way to feed a cat.

The Pickle Promenade

Jeff Baird

Pickles. Now there's a vile-sounding word if ever I heard one. The only thing worse than the sound is the taste, or maybe the smell. No wait—it's the look.

Well, whatever it is, pickles are the devil's tool. For as long as I can remember, they have been the bane of my culinary existence. Wow, I am feeling queasy just thinking about them.

I don't know where the "Pickle Phobia" came from. I suppose it could be because of my Redheaded Gene—or might be related to my younger years and the tale of "Peter Piper" and how he "picked a peck of pickled peppers." I cringe as I remember the old days at the dinner table where I would be forced to eat everything on my plate, which, of course, included Pickles. Simultaneously reciting the nursery rhyme about that Peter guy, over and over and over, I imagined him leering, saying, "I've got your 'Pickled Peppers' right here, just waiting for you!"

Possibly I would be able to function normally if I were not bombarded on a daily basis by this green monstrosity. They say that positive visualization is a technique that can be helpful for certain types of phobias. The problem is that every time I eat out, I positively visualize the waitress or the cook infecting my plate with Pickle juice. I must be wearing the scarlet letter "P." Any time I go out for a meal, I have to plead with the waitress to leave off the pickle garnish, emphasizing that if I see or smell pickles on my dish, I will be sending it back, not only for fresh food, but for a clean plate.

I can only imagine the goings-on in the kitchen after the numerous times I have sent back food, due to my "Pickle Phobia." It probably goes something like this: The waitress arrives back in the kitchen with the pickle garnish topping the untouched food platter. The cook asks, "Why didn't he just take it off the plate?" The waitress explains sarcastically, between blowing bubbles, that she already tried that. Then the cook, after putting my food on a clean dish, gets the pickle juice out and brushes my burger with "Pickle Venom" spouting: "Pickle this!" (Actually, having also worked in the restaurant industry for many years, I believe that brushing my burger with pickle juice is the least of my worries.)

Then we begin the dance of the "Pickle Promenade" as the waitress brings the food back to me. Most of the time, I can see the cooks gathering by the windows nearest my table so that they can witness the upcoming show. I would venture a guess that they have a "Pickle Pool" running in the kitchen to see how long it will take me to get the look—you know the one I am talking about: the "Pickle Pucker."

Like in old movies, the plate is set down in front of me, the waitress looks at me, I look at her, she turns to look back to the kitchen where all eyes are trained on me. If I am dining with someone, they look at me, then the waitress, then the kitchen, and the whole process starts over. It's like watching heads move back and forth at a tennis match.

The waitress and I both know that someone has done something to my plate in retaliation for my demands. But the dance must continue towards its inevitable conclusion. Because, above all else, I am ultimately a "Pickle Weenie," and abhor confrontation.

I put on my biggest and most hapless "Howdy Dowdy" grin. I thank the waitress while explaining that I am deathly allergic to pickles, and if one even comes near my food, I could die. It's a lie—a little green lie—but the dance must continue. If this were a movie, there would be a foreboding piano piece playing in the background leading up to a crescendo of the "Dill Pickle Rag."

I take a bite. I move the food around on my tongue. The waitress stands by, watching, when under any other circumstances she would have left to serve another party by then.

At first it tastes okay—even good. But then, from out of nowhere, there it is. PICKLE JUICE!

I cough, spit the food out onto my plate, and hold my breath so that I turn Redhead Red in the face. I grab my throat like a man choking to death. The waitress turns white, and the cook runs out of the kitchen yelling, "Is there a doctor in the house?"

I wave him off, and cough a few more times saying that it wasn't a big enough dose, and I should survive. As I wipe my tongue with my napkin, the cook whisks my plate away and apologizes profusely for allowing my food to be in the same kitchen as a pickle. He assures me he will make up something fresh—anything I want. How about a nice juicy steak? And, of course, sir, it's all on the house.

There've been times over the years when I have felt guilty about the wasted food and the rolled eyes of the wait staff as they thought I was joking. But no more. My feelings have hardened just like the thick outer hideous skin of an extra-large Pickle. I now stand up for my rights and hope my modest efforts give someone else the courage to stand up and just say "No" to Pickles. If I can prevent just one senseless "Pickle Mishap," then I will feel that, in some small way, I have contributed to the righting of a grievous wrong.

The free steaks are nice, too.

Nectar of the Gods

Ralph Hieb

"Run, Jimmy!" Tommy yelled.

"I am!"

Tommy risked a glance behind. The furious swarm of bees seemed closer.

"Whose idea was this?" Jimmy wailed.

"Just keep running."

"The stream. Jump into the water."

Both boys jumped into the stream. Holding their breath, they stayed under water for as long as their lungs could stand.

Emerging after what they thought of as an eternity, they peeked cautiously, eyes slightly above the water before crawling onto the bank opposite from where they jumped in.

"Who would have thought those bees would get so mad if we tried to take some honey?" Jimmy said, looking up at Tommy.

"I read in my history book that the ancients called it the nectar or the gods." Tommy, looked down at his kid brother. "Maybe they had beekeepers or someone who was a bee whisperer."

"What's a bee whisperer?" Jimmy asked.

"You know. Like a horse whisperer. Only he talks to bees."

"You're nuts. There ain't no such thing."

"Then how'd they do it?"

"I don't know," Tommy answered wringing the water from his t-shirt. "Look it up in the library."

"Okay. Let's head home," Jimmy said as he tried sliding his shoes in the grass. "I need to get this mud off before we get home."

"What happened to you two?" their mother asked when they walked through the back door into the kitchen. "You're tracking water and mud over my freshly waxed floor."

"Sorry, Mom," Tommy said.

"Yeah, Mom. Sorry. We was just trying to get some honey and the bees didn't like it," Jimmy added.

"Great," Mom said. "Go outside and take off those wet things and leave your shoes outside," she said.

"You need to talk to your father when he gets home," Mom added as she grabbed a mop to clean the floor.

"I guess we're in trouble," Jimmy said to Tommy.

"Yeah. I guess so."

～ᢒ

That night, when Dad arrived home from work, their mother said that the boys wanted to talk to him.

After the brothers retold their tale of the afternoon's adventure, they waited for their father to get mad.

"Well," Dad began. "Nectar of the gods is also called ambrosia. And it's not necessarily honey. It was the food that the gods of ancient Greece and Rome desired most. Why do you want the nectar of the gods?"

"There's this girl at school who's real weak and can't walk," Tommy answered. "Her name is Wendy."

"And Tommy thinks that it can help her," added Jimmy.

"I'm sure the doctors are doing whatever needs to be done to help her," Dad said, his hand on Tommy's shoulder. "Now I think you both need to get ready for bed."

"I guess," Tommy said. He walked to his bedroom and mumbled "I'm not gonna give up. I'll find that stuff to make her better."

Ten years later . . .

"Hey Jim," Mom called. "Tell your father dinner's ready."

Sitting down at the dinner table Dad asked, "Where's Tom?"

"Guess," Jim answered.

"You know perfectly well, Dean," Mom said.

"Over at Wendy's," he answered.

"He's still trying to talk her into going to the senior prom with him," Mom said.

"At least he has given up on finding," Dad held up his fingers to give quotes, "the nectar of the gods."

Jim shook his head, stabbing into another slice of meat loaf. "Tom will never give up on his hunt."

Mom sighed. "Dean. This nectar thing is turning into an unhealthy obsession. You need to talk to him."

"Yes dear," said Dean, slicing into his meatloaf.

Eight years later . . .

"I've heard that you have the genuine nectar of the gods," Tom said.

"My boy, I have no idea what you are referring to," replied the old man as he brushed a few strands of long gray hair from in front of his face.

"You know. The drink the gods of ancient times used to make them stronger."

"I believe the nectar was the tastiest drink they knew of. So it was only for the gods," the old man said, leaning back in his chair and folding his hands over a well-rounded stomach. "But it is nothing more than a myth."

"I know it's not a myth," Tom said. "I've been looking for twenty years. I know it will help my wife walk again."

"I can appreciate your goal, but I am afraid you've been misled." The old man cleared his throat reached in front of him and took a drink from the mug sitting on the table. "If the nectar could cure people with handicaps, then I am quite certain people would have been seeking it for all the centuries since it first appeared in tales." He set down his mug. "I can guarantee the nectar referred to in ancient legends is honey. Have you tried that?"

"I've tried honey and everything in the world of herbs and spices, but nothing works," Tom said, frustrated. "If I brought Wendy here, you would see that she can be cured." Tom's voice turned pleading. "Please help us."

The old man slowly nodded his head, relenting. "I will look at the young lady; however, I cannot promise anything. What you seek does not exist."

"It does exist," Tom insisted.

"Very well. Bring her to this address tomorrow night," the old man said, handing Tom a business card. "And it must be dark outside. Do not tell anyone where you are going."

⁓

As Tom parked the car, he looked around at the parking lot with its weeds growing through the broken pavement. Before them, a dilapidated mall stood as a gray blotch against the horizon.

"Are you sure this is where we're supposed to go?" Wendy asked.

"Yeah," Tom answered, as he removed her wheelchair from the back of the hatchback.

"It smells of decaying things."

Tom hadn't noticed until she mentioned it. He kept looking around at the deserted parking lot. It surrounded the old shopping mall that had been abandoned years earlier.

"I remember coming here when I was a kid," Wendy said. "They had a medical supply store. It's where I got my first wheelchair."

"My mom used to take Jim and me here for clothes shopping before school," Tom said, as he headed to a door with a number on it. He was surprised to see that this area had the weeds and trash removed.

The door squeaked loudly as Tom pushed it open. Using his back to hold the door, Tom pulled Wendy's wheelchair into the dimly-lit area.

As the door slowly closed, both Tom and Wendy could feel the dampness in the air.

"Which way do we go?" Tom said as his eyes adjusted to the dim light.

"I don't know," Wendy answered. "I'm scared. Let's just leave."

"I'm starting to think this was a stupid idea," Tom said looking around nervously.

"Wait," Wendy sniffed. "Do you smell that?"

"The stink of rotting things, yeah it's pretty bad."

"No. I mean like bread baking."

Tom stopped from turning the chair toward the exit. He inhaled then tried to peer further down the long expanse that stretched into darkness. "I smell it now."

"Someone else is in here with us, and they're baking something," said Wendy.

"It took you two long enough to smell the bread."

Tom and Wendy faced the direction of the voice.

"Who are you?" Tom asked.

"Your guide." A woman stepped out from the shadows.

"Our guide?" Wendy asked.

"I am told by Malcolm that you seek the nectar of the gods." She looked at them for confirmation.

"Yes," Tom answered.

"Then I will lead you to it."

"You mean there really is such a thing?" Wendy asked, a surprise in her voice.

"Definitely," the woman replied.

"Malcolm, that's the old man I talked to," Tom said.

"Yes. Would you care for some fresh baked rolls with honey?"

"Excuse me," Wendy said as the woman led them to a softly lit room along the corridor. "I didn't catch your name."

"My apologies," the woman said. "It is Gabrielle. Please, Tom, have some bread or rolls. They are quite delicious. If you do not care for honey, we have fresh made jellies and jams. It is all quite good. While you eat, I will just take Wendy to the back where she can try the nectar of the gods."

Before Tom could think of a response, Gabrielle took hold of Wendy's wheelchair, and they disappeared through a side door. It closed with a final sounding click.

Running to the door, Tom found it locked. He pounded on it. "Bring her back." When he got no response, he sank to the floor crying. Strangled sobs of, "bring my wife back," flowed through the twilight of the room.

⌒

Tom awoke to the smells of more fresh-baked rolls and newly-brewed coffee. Through half-closed eyes, he saw the figure of a person standing in the room. It bent over him.

"You have been asleep for almost three days," Gabrielle informed him.

"Wendy," Tom muttered. "Where is Wendy?"

"She is doing quite well. Her response to the nectar is extremely satisfactory." Gabrielle smiled and walked to a door against the far wall. "We moved you here when you fell asleep. I think this room is far better suited to rest than the floor of the corridor where we first met." She stepped through the door, closing it behind her.

Tom stood to follow then realized he was naked. "Where

are my clothes!" he yelled falling back to sit on the edge of a king-size bed. Looking around the room, he spied his clothes hanging from a clothes tree in one corner.

After getting dressed, Tom went through the door. *Which way do I go?* Sniffing the air, he stopped. *Fresh baked bread.* Following the aroma, Tom came to the old food court.

He stood, transfixed at the scene. A group of women were busy baking with industrial-sized ovens, using the old tables as cooling racks. A sign on the wall read *Mama Vee's Homemade Breads.* Tom knew the name; it was a popular brand at upscale restaurants and boutique food stores.

"It is something to see," Gabrielle said from behind him. "I believe you know the brand."

"Yes, I do. I have to stock it on the shelves where I work." Tom said turning to her. "Where is Wendy? I want to see her now," he demanded.

"I was just coming to take you to her." Gabrielle smiled, displaying perfect white teeth. "Please follow me." She turned and led the way back down the hall toward a door that blended into the wall.

Walking through the doorway, Tom was amazed at the difference in how everything appeared. The hall was wide with tasteful art on the walls. The floors had hardwood with a long carpet runner in designs of red and royal blue. Following Gabrielle further along, he saw that the doors were spaced at greater distances, similar to how an apartment building would be.

"She is in this room," Gabrielle said, opening a door.

Tom walked in and saw Wendy sitting in her wheelchair. Running to her he asked. "Hon, are you all right? I was worried. They said I was out for a couple of days. What happened?" The questions rushed from him.

"Slow down and give me a chance to speak," Wendy said. "Do you like this room? It's ours."

"We have an apartment," Tom said. "This is nice, but we don't live here. Let's just get out of here."

"I've accepted a position here. And you can have a job

delivering the bread to their customers."

"I don't need a new job."

"It's the easiest way. This way we can be together."

"We are together. You're my wife. What's gotten into you?"

Wendy gestured around the room. "But here we would never have to worry about paying bills or any of the other worries we had before."

She stood up.

"You're standing," Tom said. Tears welled up. The nectar had worked!

"Yes, and I like it here."

As she turned, the gleam of pure white fangs glistened from her mouth. "Gabrielle gave me the true nectar of the gods; now I am going to share with you."

Tom stood rigid as Wendy slowly walked closer, her mouth a gaping maw.

Tom inched backward away from, "Wendy don't. What have they done to you?"

She smiled and continued moving toward him.

"I love you. Please stop," Tom pleaded.

"I know," Wendy said smiling. "Now I will return that love with the gift of the true nectar."

She grabbed Tom with hands stronger than any that he had ever felt. Pulling him closer, she gently placed her mouth to his neck. "Relax," she whispered. "When I'm finished with you, you will know the joy of the nectar. Then we can spend forever together."

He looked pleadingly into her glowing red eyes. Unable to move he whimpered slightly and closed his eyes turning his head from her.

Her bite was sharp and clean, as she drank the nectar of the gods.

Recipe for Disaster

A. E. Decker

"You know this is wrong," said Jude's Good Angel.

Jude took the Tabasco sauce out of the refrigerator door. While he was there, he cracked open a cold Dos Equis. Swigged. "Ah."

"And now you're drinking." The angel's nose wrinkled. "You do realize it's not even noon?"

"Shut up," said Jude, slamming the refrigerator door.

Most people have a Bad Angel perched on their other shoulder to balance out the Good One. In Jude's case, the Powers that Be had declared a Bad Angel redundant. If the world possessed a self-destruct button sealed away behind locked doors, Jude would be the one to drug the dogs, scale the gates, crack the code, and press it before the paint on the warning sign dried.

And then, when the first explosions began fracturing the world, he'd say: "I just wanted to see what would happen."

As his Good Angel watched, scowling disapprovingly, Jude took the Tabasco to a large Tupperware bowl set on the counter and peered at the mixture coagulating inside. The substance was lumpy, yet shiny, possessing the consistency of both sand and snot. It *glooped.* Jude added a teaspoon of Tabasco then picked up a wooden spoon and thrust it into the center of the glop.

He stirred twice then, experimentally, let go of the spoon. It stood straight up.

Then it began dissolving. Jude raised an eyebrow. "Huh."

"See?" said the angel.

The last inch of spoon vanished into the batter. The gloop made thoughtful smacking sounds, as if dissatisfied with the spoon's flavor.

"Guess I'll need the mixer," said Jude.

"No!" wailed the angel. "Just stop it now!"

Jude fetched the mixer, experiencing a thrill of pride when he remembered to lower the beaters into the bowl before turning it on. Usually he gave himself an impromptu batter-bath. The beaters whipped the mixture into the consistency of pureed frogs. They also corroded, but that was okay. Jude dropped them in the sink just as the oven's buzzer went off. Six-hundred and sixty-six degrees.

I remembered to preheat the oven, too. Jude's dagger-shaper earring swung with an extra-jaunty swish as he retrieved the greased 9x9 baking pan from the stovetop. He picked up the bowl.

"Don't," begged the angel, tugging Jude's shirt as he tipped the bowl over the pan. "Pour it in the sink. The drain needs unclogging anyway."

The batter slid reluctantly down the side of the tilted bowl then changed its mind and dropped all at once, landing with a faint squelch. It lay in the pan like overturned road kill, exposing a sallow, faintly pebbled underside. Jude smoothed it into the pan's corners with a spatula then tossed the spatula in the trash when it split down the center. The Good Angel wailed as he placed the pan in the oven and set the timer for six minutes.

"That should do it," said Jude, leaning back against the sink. He took another swig of beer. The angel shot him a hostile glower and crouched on the oven handle, head sunk into his shoulders.

The curious, acrid scent of marshmallows poached in rotten vinegar seeped from the oven, growing in intensity as the minutes ticked off the clock. Wrinkling his nose, Jude rubbed the cross-shaped scar on his left cheek—shooting himself with a staple gun hadn't been his best idea. Interesting experience, though.

Now there was a hint of burnt gym shoes to the odor. "Phew," said Jude. "Is it supposed to smell like that?" Frowning, he checked the timer. One minute left. . . .

Without warning, the house quaked. Jude rocked back, smacking hard against the sink's edge. The stained kitchen tiles cracked and separated, emitting puffs of boiling green steam.

"What the . . .?" cried Jude, clinging to the sink. Another violent ripple shook the room, shifting cabinets and opening drawers. Pots spilled across the floor.

"'*What the?*' he asks." Still riding the oven handle like a bumper car, the Good Angel rolled his eyes to the ceiling. "I know you can read, Jude. I know you read this." Fluttering over to an empty box sitting on the counter, the Good Angel shook tiny fists at the blaring red letters printed over every side. APOCALYPSE BROWNIES. WARNING: DO NOT BAKE.

Jude swallowed. "I just wanted to see what would happen."

Outside, the sky blackened. It also began to smell of fish.

"Well, hurrah for you, Jude," screamed the angel. "I'll tell you what's going to happen. The world's going to end, all because of your . . ."

Good Angels don't curse, so what followed was the aural equivalent of a trail of soapy bubbles primly muted by a shimmering pink haze.

". . . curiosity," finished the angel.

End? Jude stood blinking. Slowly, the word settled in his mind, interlocking with memories of past schemes gone horribly wrong. Like the time he'd thought it would be fun to put on an Obama mask and drive through an NRA convention yelling: *"I'm coming to take your guns away!"*

But this was worse. This was—end? The world couldn't end yet. Not when there were still so many interesting bits left for him to muck with.

"Jude, the timer's going to go off in thirty seconds!"

For once, his Good Angel's cry galvanized Jude. Grabbing a glove, he dove at the oven and wrestled with the handle. The door creaked open half an inch before sticking fast. Something inside the oven chuckled richly. Wafts of Stygian smoke seeped greasily out of the crack and pooled on the cracked kitchen tiles. Jude turned his head aside to cough. Blue sparks singed his forearms.

"Jude, hurry!" cried the angel.

Jude dragged in one great, egg-stinking, deep breath then set a boot against a drawer for extra leverage. Both shoulders popped as he pulled, groaning between his teeth.

"Ten seconds!" The angel danced from foot to foot on the stovetop.

Black lightning cracked the windows. Jude's last unchipped plate fell off a shelf and broke. Still Jude strained. "Help me," he croaked.

The angel's blink of surprise used up another two seconds. Then he swooped down from the stove and added his small strength to Jude's. Together, as the last seconds ticked down, they heaved the oven door open just as the timer let out an obscene bleat.

"Too late!" cried the angel. A glowing figure squatted on the oven rack, seemingly composed all of fire and smoke and deep, awful stench. It chortled; a bone-melting sound.

"Too late, hell," said Jude. Channeling the ghosts of bar brawls past, he grabbed up his beer bottle and threw it into the oven.

The figure paused. It ran a forked tongue over its blue lips.

Jude glared. "That was my last Dos Equis, asshole."

The figure belched. Then belched again, yellow eyes bugging. A flare of yeasty-smelling fire erupted from its mouth, licking out to consume the creature whole. Jude clung to the sink as the kitchen shook like a funhouse floor, the angel swaying on his shoulder.

Then, with a final hiccough, everything settled.

Jude looked at the angel. The angel fluttered to the oven.

Dipping a finger into the crusty mess still bubbling inside the baking pan, he brought it to his mouth.

A soft smack of lips.

Jude straightened. "Always suspected beer could save the world," he said. He slicked back his hair and brushed ash off his shoulders.

"No," said the angel. "It wasn't the beer." He turned with a smile, wings un-bunching. "You left out the baking soda. Thank goodness you flunked home economics."

"I skipped home eco—wait." Jude stopped brushing. "You mean I wasted my last Dos Equis for nothing?"

"Serves you right, drinking before noon." Beaming, the angel spread his wings. "I think saving the world deserves a nice cup of milky tea, don't you?" Jumping into the air, he turned a cartwheel into a wisp of ether and vanished.

Grumbling, Jude pulled off the oven glove and dropped it in the sink. Thirteen gallons of water later, it finally stopped smoking. Jude shut off the faucet then, slouching, turned to survey his shattered kitchen. The empty brownie box sat on the counter, the neon letters on its label screaming a warning that could be read a hundred paces off.

"Didn't even get the recipe right," Jude muttered, picking it up.

Didn't get it right . . . He flapped the box thoughtfully against his hand. His lips pursed.

"I wonder if the supermarket has any more of these?"

The King's Potatoes

Jerry McFadden

Joachim sat in the dreary cell, waiting to be executed. The turnkeys would open the massive iron door late in the afternoons to read the list of names. A few of the men would stand up quickly, clanking their ankle and wrist shackles, as if anxious to get it over, infinitely tired of the waiting. Others would squirm away, scuttling into the corner shadows or ducking behind their fellow prisoners. Then the jailers would come after them with their ugly short whips, driving them into the open.

The barred windows were too high for anyone to see out. But they could watch the fading light of the late afternoon and hear the rattle of chains as the men shuffled across the courtyard, followed by the shouted orders that hurried the soldiers into position. Then a beat of silence, interrupted only by the murmur of the priest. The prayers were cut short by the harsh commands of, "Ready, aim, fire." Everyone in the cell, in spite of their anticipation, would flinch at the volley of musket fire. The choking smell of gunfire would then drift in through the windows, along with the sounds of mules and wagons and work details taking away the dead.

Joachim did not know how he would react when his name was called. Would he have the courage to stand up, to calmly say, "*Si, 'stoy aqui*; I am Joachim Inbanez," then walk out to death like a man? Or would he huddle back against the wall and make them come after him? None of his fellow prisoners would care one way or other. He would be forgotten by the following afternoon when other names were called.

This afternoon, much to everyone's surprise, the turnkeys returned an hour after the executions. A nobleman in fine clothes strode into the room, holding a perfumed scarf over his nose to ward off the stench of stale sweat from the mass of bodies, the rotten food scattered on the floor, the streaks of urination fouling the walls, and the feces overflowing from scattered buckets. The men moved aside for him as he walked through the crowd as if he were carrying the plague.

He moved through the horde, stopping occasionally to point at a man, saying, "Stand up."

The man would stand.

The nobleman would stare distastefully at him a long moment, before saying: "Stay standing," or "Sit back down." He would then push further along.

He'd collected three men when he eyed Joachim. He no longer needed to speak. He pointed his finger, and Joachim stood up. He walked away to select two more men. "Bring them," he finally said to the guards, turning to walk out of the cell.

The six men trundled after him, flanked by their jailers, through a series of tunnels before entering a windowless room that was obviously a workshop. A huge bald man in a leather apron waited for them. One by one, they stretched their chains across his anvil, and the man banged the rivets off with clean, brutal strokes of a sledgehammer.

The men remained silent, rubbing their wrists and ankles, searching one another's eyes, as if another might have the answer to what was going on. The nobleman came back into the room. When he was satisfied that the chains were gone, he said, "*Venga*; come."

They walked across the courtyard. The King's soldiers stared at them curiously, without malice, watching them being led into another windowless room. A woman waited for them this time, with a pile of clean clothes. Other women were pouring buckets of hot water into two large tubs. "Wash yourselves," the woman said. "Then put these clothes on. We will be back shortly, so do not delay."

The hot water and soap felt sensual, a forgotten pleasure, like being caressed with silk cloth. The clothes fit, more or less, and there were even boots, that also fit, more or less.

Again the nobleman came for them. Again they paraded across the courtyard. But this time they were taken into a grand room with windows and a long table with benches on both sides. Metal plates and utensils lined each side of the table. The nobleman smiled at them, actually smiled at them, and said, "Sit."

A side door opened, and a meal was carried in. Each man received only one morsel of the meal. One had soup, another had broccoli, another had a slice of meat, another had a potato, another man had pudding, and the last man had a sip of wine from an open decanter.

When they finished, the nobleman clapped his hands and told them to stand up and follow him. He took them to a small cell that had six cots. Saying nothing else, he locked the door and walked away. Every few minutes a guard would come by, open the door to survey them, saying nothing, then leave, only to come back a short time later to survey them again.

And the days followed.

Eating, resting, being surveyed, eating again, being surveyed again. At night, they were woken at intervals, made to stand up, then told to go back to bed. All of it starting over the following morning. No man ate more than a morsel of the food. One bite, two at the most, before the meal was taken away. Any effort to try for more was rewarded with a slap or a beating. They were always hungry, goaded on by the taste and smell of the food they were barely eating. The small bites, three or four times a day, did not fill their stomachs and the tantalizing odors of the meats and vegetables and roasted potatoes covered with the accompanying sauces drew them into fantasies of huge, succulent meals that they would gorge on until their bellies burst. Once a week they would go back for a bath and be given clean clothes.

They knew what was going on. They were food tasters for the King. Nothing would reach the King's mouth without first passing by them.

One night Manuel Diego said, "I cannot do this anymore."

Joachim smiled. "You would rather be shot?"

"I cannot stand the suspense of knowing that I might be eating poisoned food, that I might die after the next bite."

Joachim pointed to the door, "Then tell them to take you back to the big cell. There you can eat stale bread and rotten meat and be certain that you will soon be shot. That will alleviate the suspense."

"But here I will die in defense of the King. I am here because I joined the revolution to do away with the King."

Joachim sighed. "You knew you might die when you joined. Now, if you want to be shot, that is your choice. But here you will die clean, in clothes that do not stink. And you may die by starvation before you are poisoned."

Manuel Diego went back to sleep. In the morning, there was no more talk of being shot.

One day, in the bathroom, Joachim was surprised when a woman slipped him a small leather pouch and a note without being seen by the guards. He tucked both into his clothes without reaction, looking blandly around him as he usually did.

He read the note later in their small cell. It said *The poison will be in the potatoes.* Joachim stuck the note in his mouth, chewing it carefully before swallowing.

He became the potato man. He rudely took the potatoes away from Manuel Diego the first time. The potatoes were routinely brought to him by the waiters after that. The other men never questioned him nor spoke about it.

He would bite into the potatoes and pretend to chew, desperately trying not to swallow, trapping the slices of potatoes between his teeth and the back of his cheek. He would spit them furtively into the pouch as soon as he could without being seen, then empty it into the feces bucket where no one would look, quickly rinsing his mouth out from their communal bucket of water. But he was becoming so hungry he knew he was losing his strength and slipping in and out of delirium.

And then, one late afternoon, there was a hue and cry throughout the fort and castle. "The King is dead," people shouted. "The King is dead."

The nobleman came to the room. He stared angrily at the six men and finally said, "I do not know how you did this, but you did. The King was poisoned—from the very food you ate. You will die for this. You will all be shot tomorrow."

Joachim's five friends looked around at each other, then back at Joachim, then down at the floor. They knew. They had seen Joachim furtively emptying the small pouch into the feces bucket. Everyone else had switched foods to provide a little variety for one another, except for Joachim and the potatoes. No one had spoken of it, but they knew. But all five remained silent.

Joachim stepped forward. "I did this. Not them. There is no reason to shoot these men when I am the culprit."

"It does not matter. You were all going to die anyway, by poison or by the firing squad. We might as well do it now. The cooks have already been shot."

Joachim shrugged. "May I ask a favor?"

The nobleman stared at him in astonishment. "You dare ask me for a favor?"

"I would like to die clean. May we all have a bath one more time before we die?"

The nobleman's face colored in anger, but he found the strength to calm himself and said, "You have acted bravely. I can accept that. You may bathe this evening, for the last time, and you will all be shot at dawn."

They were taken to the baths as promised, under heavy guard. They stood silently, watching the water being poured. To their surprise, the woman came back into the room with another set of clean clothes, as was the usual procedure. Joachim nodded as he accepted his, saying the words so low that no one else could hear. "The potatoes were good."

The woman looked at him but did not acknowledge his words. She gazed at his eyes for a long moment before turning away.

As Dawn Brightens

Paul Weidknecht

Morning was still gray with fog when the boy walked down to the harbor. A bigger boy had taken his favorite sleeping spot last night, and he had not slept well, so he started this day early. He passed the closed shops and quiet rooms just above them, as yellow lights came on in some of the upstairs windows, silhouetting the rising people, stealing their mystery.

A rounded nub of black bread lay between the sea-misted cobblestones at his feet. He reached down. How had it lasted the whole night? he thought. Something or someone should have eaten it. In the past, he had eaten pieces this small, but instead he closed his hand around it and changed direction.

Soon he came to the pier where his father and mother had taken him before the war. He and his father would stand at the end and throw bread into the air for the seagulls, while his mother smiled, bundling herself against the breeze. The birds would dip in, snaring the pieces in flight. The boy wondered why God had allowed his parents to go away. One evening during supper, men carrying rifles knocked roughly on their door and spoke to his father about joining the army. The boy was confused that they did not wear uniforms like regular soldiers.

His father nodded to the men, his mother wept to herself. She filled a knapsack with clothes, cheese, and slices of dried meat, wiping the tears with the back of her wrist. Five months later his mother disappeared after one of her trips to the village to meet with the secret men. He did not like when his mother would leave, but he knew she had to meet with the secret agents because they had important information about where his father was to be found. Even though she brought home a burlap sack bulging with food, his mother was always sad because the agents never had any news. The boy thought that perhaps this last time his mother had received some special report and that she was still busy investigating. Sometimes he imagined his father and mother on a trail in the forest at night, hand in hand, working their way back to him, using the stars to guide them.

Only two gulls bobbed on the water below him; their wings neatly folded away. They did not take to the air, even when he used a trick his father had taught him, moving his arm up and down, pretending to throw bread to get the birds to gather around him. He tossed the bread and one gull ate it off the water, the other too late.

As he walked back up the pier, he thought about miracles, the kind in which people got food from heaven. He wondered if things like that happened today. A wave slapped loudly against the pilings, and he glanced down. The silver fish foundered on its side in the shallows, mouth popping open for a gulp of water, flaps flaring on the exhale, dark red gills inside. It was longer than the boy's leg, as thick as his thigh, perhaps injured or stunned; he was unsure. He ran until he found a spot low enough to jump into the water. The boy crashed through the shallows and grabbed the fish's tail with both hands. The muscles along its flanks shivered. Hunched, he dragged the fish backward, the sand running around his heels and back out to sea with the receding wash. The fish thrashed, its hard tail fin scraping into the boy's palms, as he continued wading, step by step, back to land. The fish's scales were hard, smooth, slick. The boy adjusted his grip and fell.

Gone. When the fish escaped, it swam just beyond the boy's reach and stopped, hovering there to rest. The boy stared at his palms, then balled them into fists. His arms shook as he slowly opened his hands and took a gentle step toward the fish. He stretched forward and touched the point of the tail fin. The fish kicked away with a shudder, disappearing into deeper water.

Climbing from the sea, the boy pulled off his shirt, wringing it out, splattering the cobblestones. He draped the shirt around his neck and began walking past the shops again, his pants heavy with saltwater.

"Kiro, have you fed my birds?"

The boy turned in the direction of the voice. He saw nothing.

"Kiro, up here."

He looked up.

The woman leaned through the second story window, her forearms resting on the sill. She was pale and thin-faced, like nearly everyone had become during the war, wearing a faded blue kerchief that covered most of her short brown hair.

"You were out on the pier with my birds. I own them. Remember my paper from the Ministry saying so? So I ask again, have you fed my birds?"

He remembered his mother telling him how the war had made some people crazy, especially those who had lost loved ones. She also said they were to be pitied, but that he should say nothing to them. Over these years he had heard much strange talk, and this woman claiming she owned the seagulls did not scare him, so he answered.

"Yes."

"Good, now come up and eat. Your breakfast is getting cold. And we will get you out of those wet clothes."

As he walked to the shopfront door that led upstairs he wondered if this person Kiro had been her son, someone whom she had loved, then lost to the war. When he tried the door, it was locked, but when he heard the woman coming down the wooden steps, he smiled. She might know some things, he thought, like where to meet the secret agents. And she might know what forest his father and mother were in, what trail they were on, and what star was guiding them.

Chicken Flautas

Emily P. W. Murphy

Three mornings after we buried my mother, I woke craving her chicken flautas. Not in twenty years, since I carried my daughter, Julie, had I felt such an urge for anything, and never for my mother's Mexican cooking.

As a child, I preferred American food. While my mother made her own menudo, caldo de res, and of course flautas, I begged her to make hamburgers, French fries, and potato salad. Instead of *sopapillas*, I asked for cake on my birthdays. When my mother made *arroz con leche*, I'd ask for instant pudding, and when she made *flan* I wanted apple pie. When I went away to college, I delighted in the opportunity to eat spaghetti instead of homemade salsa, and baked chicken instead of mole.

When I married a white man, my mother offered to teach me the traditional cooking, but I chose instead to learn from my mother-in-law the art of dressing a turkey, and layering lasagna. Our Julie never complained. It was easy for her to eat the foods her friends knew, and she could always have the traditional dishes when she visited her grandparents.

The craving returned a week later when my father phoned.

"My friend Carlos is moving into a home." His voice sounded resolute, but sad over the phone. "He will have a one-bedroom apartment to himself, and will take his meals in a big dining room down the hall. I have decided to go, too, and be his neighbor."

I pictured my father in my mother's sunny yellow kitchen, the long-corded wall phone cupped in his callused, brown hand. I gripped my cell as I told him making such a decision so soon after Mama's death was unnecessary. "We will bring you meals." I shifted the phone to my other ear and flexed my stiff fingers. "I was thinking of making chicken flautas."

I could envision my papa's firm expression, his jaw set, and his kind eyes surrounded by lowered brows. "You make your mama's *flautas*," he said, "and bring them to my new home."

I returned the phone to my pocket and sank into a nearby chair. Mama was gone, Papa would sell my childhood home, and I didn't even know how to make chicken *flautas*. My life would never again be the same.

My longing for *flautas* grew even greater. I turned to the internet to search for a recipe. The first I found seemed fairly simple and required only seven ingredients. I jotted a grocery list on a sheet of paper, and left for the store.

Back home, I dropped my grocery bags on my black granite countertops, and took my frying pan down from the rack over the kitchen island. Propping my laptop well away from both sink and stove, I clicked over to the bookmarked recipe and read the directions.

As the oven preheated, I cooked the chicken on the stove, removing it to a plate to cool and harden once it was no longer pink. I wiped out the pan, and returned it to the stovetop, adding a tablespoon of oil to heat.

As soon as the chicken was cool enough to handle, I shredded it with my fingers. This activity brought me back to my mother's yellow kitchen, when I was too short to reach the counter without standing on a chair. Back then it was always my job to shred the cool chicken into a bowl. Why did I not continue to learn?

Wiping a tear from my eye with the back of my wrist, I glanced at the recipe. My laptop had gone to its screensaver, so I brushed my elbow over the touchpad. The next step was to combine cheese, cumin, and chicken in a bowl, so I added the ingredients and mixed the chicken with my hands.

When the oil on the stovetop was hot, I fried the flat tortillas, removed them from the oil, added the filling, and rolled them into flutes. Transferring them to a cookie sheet, I set them in the oven to bake. While something about this process seemed right, I could not shake the feeling that this was not how my mother had cooked so many years ago—before I stopped paying attention. The *flautas* finished baking just as my husband returned home.

"Hey honey," he said, walking into the kitchen. "Whatcha cooking? It smells good."

"I am attempting my mother's chicken *flautas*," I said, turning off the oven, and opening the door to show him.

His forehead creased. "Not too spicy, I hope." My husband had no taste for spice.

"No, not too spicy," I assured him, though I didn't really know.

We sat together at the table and each tried the *flautas*. Even before I got the first bite past my lips, I knew the recipe was wrong. The smell, texture, and taste were not even close to what I remembered.

"Well, what do you think?" I asked my husband, as I tried to hide my disappointment.

He made a face. "Are you sure this is the same recipe?" He poked at the *flautas* on his plate with his salad fork.

I shook my head. "I hoped it would be, but no."

He took a deep breath and put the fork down. "Oh good.

Because these are nothing like hers. I think you might have the seasoning wrong."

I sighed and stood up to clear the table and call for pizza. "I think I have everything wrong," I said, and went into the kitchen to drop the *flautas* into the trash.

My failure did not quell my craving, and two days later, I searched the internet for another recipe. I soon found that while the recipe I tried called for baking the *flautas*, most recipes required frying them, using the oven only to keep them warm. This seemed right, somehow. It felt natural to roll the *flautas* before placing them in the oil. The new recipes called for more vegetables and spices, which also seemed right.

Still, I did not wish to subject my husband to another failure, so I waited until a night he had to work late to try again. This time, I used all fresh ingredients: homemade salsa, peppers, onions, cilantro, and lime. I gathered the spices in the recipe, and cooked and shredded the chicken. I felt as if my mother were standing behind me, dressed in her favorite red dress with her perfect white apron. I closed my eyes and was by the sink in the yellow kitchen, gazing out the window to my mother's garden, and breathing the fragrances of hot oil and spices. When I opened my eyes and took in my stainless steel appliances, I knew the smells from my memory did not match those of the present. Surely the seasoning was once again wrong.

Still, I followed the recipe, frying the flautas, and setting them to warm in the oven. When I sat down to taste, I had to admit that the results were closer to my mother's cooking, though, as I suspected, the spices were not the same.

My craving did not diminish. I longed not for flautas, but for *her flautas*. I channeled my disappointment into determination.

Perhaps the secret to my mother's *flautas* was not in the filling, but in the tortilla. I remembered seeing her make tortillas from scratch, but could not be certain whether she had then used those same tortillas to make *flautas*. I searched for a tortilla recipe, and that weekend, I promised myself, I would make my own.

While my husband watched a football game in the den, I gathered the ingredients on my granite counter. Pulling my long black hair to the back of my head with a plastic clip, I read the instructions for tortillas. They seemed simple, just *masa de maiz* and water. I followed the recipe as well as I could, but without a tortilla press, my tortillas turned out nothing like those in the picture. Perhaps with practice I could emulate my mother's perfect circles, but my shapeless blobs were far from what I desired. Still, despite the sweat dripping down my face, my gooey rolling pin, and the layer of corn flour coating my entire kitchen, in the end I had a handful of acceptable tortillas to turn into *flautas*.

I repeated the second recipe, adjusting the spices to try to create the remembered scent, but even with the homemade tortillas, the *flautas* were not the same. Five hours, and one very messy kitchen later, I was no closer to my mother's *flautas* than I had been the day she died. The tears that pricked my eyes had nothing to do with freshly chopped onion.

I spent the next week ignoring the craving. I cooked all my usual dishes—lasagna, baked macaroni and cheese, meatloaf, and vegetable stew—but in the back of my mind, the chicken *flautas* remained. At night I would dream I was in the yellow kitchen, with my mother. I would wrap my arms around her and smell her perfume, and say, "I'm so glad you're all right! I missed you so much!" and she would laugh and hug me back and say, "How would you like some chicken *flautas?*"

I always woke up just as she placed her frying pan on the stove, and the sadness of her loss washed over and through me.

My father did not falter in his resolution to move, and soon he phoned to request my help with my mother's belongings. "I will take very little to the home," he told me. "And I can pack my own things. But only you will know what of your mother's to keep, and what to sell or give away."

Only my love for my Papa made it possible for me to drive over to do as he asked. How I wished we could keep my childhood home just as it had always been, keep my mother's dresses in her closet, and the yellow kitchen as she left it.

I parked in my parents' driveway and walked around the house to enter through the back kitchen door, just as I had every day after school as a girl. I went in without knocking and stood in the kitchen. The yellow of the walls was still bright, the white curtains framing the window as crisp as they were in my earliest memory. I could still smell my mother's perfume.

Outside of the kitchen, everything had changed.

In the hall, there were packed boxes everywhere, some marked "move," others "Goodwill." I tried not to pay attention to the trash bags, wondering which of my precious memories my father was throwing away.

"Papa," I called from the hall in the middle of the house.

"Ah, Maribel." My father's voice was sad but strong. "I am in my room."

His words hit me in the heart. "My" room, not "our" room. At home with my husband and my granite kitchen, it was easy to pretend that my mother was still here, that she and my father were just as they ought to be. But, of course, he could not pretend.

I walked down the hall toward my father's voice, and found him sitting on his side of the old queen-sized bed. His side of the room was all boxes, but my mother's side was exactly as before, even her nightgown neatly folded on her pillow.

"Papa," I felt the sob rise unbidden from my chest. "I am so sorry."

We embraced, and I felt my father shudder as he pressed his face into my hair. Never before had I seen Papa cry. Even at my mother's funeral, while my daughter and I were fountains of grief, and my husband dabbed at his eyes, my father was the stoic patriarch; accepting condolences, but not revealing the depths of his loss.

Standing in that half room, with the future unknowable and the past all around us, I knew my father had to move. Even with the yellow kitchen right down the hall, my mother would never again be with us. The house was one of memories, no longer one of life.

Papa drew away and gestured toward Mama's side of the room. "I can't take it with me," he said.

I nodded and squeezed his hand. "I understand." I picked up one of the trash bags my father had draped over the doorknob, circled the bed, and took one last look at my mother's things before sorting them into new lives.

When the traces of my mother were packed into boxes and bags, I followed my papa to the little yellow kitchen. He lowered himself into his chair at the wooden kitchen table. "I won't have room for this in the apartment," he said, brushing his rough fingers over the worn grain. "Do you have a place for it?"

I thought of my stainless and granite kitchen and shook my head. "I'm sure we can find a place for it."

He nodded and swallowed, not meeting my eyes. I sat across the table, in "my" seat and looked around the kitchen. "I tried making Mama's *flautas de pollo*," I said, staring at the patch of sunlight hitting the wall across from the window. "I wish I'd let her teach me how."

Papa didn't answer. I looked at him. He was still studying the table, but the corners of his mouth were . . . not quite smiling. He nodded so slowly I almost didn't notice, but still said nothing.

"I've been craving them ever since . . ." I let my voice trail away.

Papa sighed and shifted in his chair, finally meeting my eyes. "She was going to make them," he said, looking down again. "That day."

"Really?" I looked around the kitchen, as if I could find her, but, of course, we were alone.

"She went to the market"—he took a deep breath--"that morning. After she put the groceries away, she said . . ." He sniffed. ". . . she was tired. She'd just lie down for a minute." He pulled an old handkerchief out of his breast pocket and blew his nose.

It didn't matter. I knew the rest.

I stood up to get Papa a glass of cold tap water. "Do you remember what she bought?" I asked as I ran the tap, my back to him. I turned and found him looking across the kitchen at the refrigerator. I took two steps to place the glass on the table next to his hand, then stepped back to lean against the sink.

"I don't know," he said, his eyes still trained on the refrigerator. "I never thought to ask."

I clasped my hands in front of me, and looked down at my thumbs. "Me either." I studied the pattern in the wlinoleum and remembered helping my mother replace that floor, square by square, when I was in high school.

"But," my father said, "if she bought it that day, it is still here."

My head jerked up. His gaze was still directed toward the fridge, but his eyes were misty and distant.

"*¿Qué, papá?*"

"I haven't been in here since . . ." He sighed. "I haven't thrown anything away."

I pushed away from the sink and crossed the small kitchen to the refrigerator. I pulled on the chrome handle and the door opened with a pop of displaced air. Foul odors surrounded me and I shut the door. Of course, it had been weeks; the food had all spoiled.

I returned to the sink and opened the cupboard below to retrieve a trash bag. Holding my breath, I opened the refrigerator door once more.

I sorted through the various unidentifiable leftovers, empty-ing the Corningware containers into the bag, and then setting them to soak in the sink. I opened the poultry drawer and pulled out the chicken, tossing it only after noting the type and amount of chicken breast. It was identical to the chicken I purchased from my local market.

I moved on to the produce drawer, pulling out bag after bag of mushy vegetables. I identified the decomposing red onion and garlic quickly. My mother always kept them together in a plastic bag, claiming cold onions didn't sting her eyes. In another produce bag, I found a shriveled lime. Another contained a moldy jalapeno. The cilantro had decomposed so completely, I knew it only by the tag that once wrapped around the stems, and now sat in a puddle of green. In the deli drawer, I found my mother's corn tortillas, store bought, not homemade, and a block of green cheddar cheese.

By the time I finished throwing away the spoiled food, the refrigerator was nearly empty. I sat back on my heels and studied the empty shelves, shaking my head.

"What is it?"

I jumped, having forgotten my father at the kitchen table. I stood, closed the refrigerator door, and turned to face him, tying a knot in the top of the trash bag.

"I don't understand." I felt tears form in my eyes. "Our ingredients are identical. The onion, the chicken, every vegetable is the same, and yet my *flautas* are different. It must be something in the seasoning."

Leaving the trash bag in the middle of the kitchen floor, I opened my mother's spice cabinet, certain I would find some exotic spice to explain my failure. But I found nothing unusual. Nothing to explain the difference.

"Papa." I turned back to him. "Do you know how Mama seasoned her *flautas?*"

My father smiled that sad echo of a smile and nodded. "She seasoned her *flautas* just as she seasoned all of her food. With love. Your mother put a part of herself into every meal she cooked for us." He looked away, and folded his hands on the table before him. "It is why nothing will ever taste the same."

I invited my father back to my house for dinner. "Julie will be home," I said to persuade him. "She comes home to do laundry every Thursday evening."

My father raised an eyebrow. "Have they no machines at the university?"

I smiled and shrugged. "Of course, but ours are free, and it is a pleasure to me to see her."

He nodded his assent. I picked up the one box I had packed to bring home with me, containing my mother's perfume, tortilla press, and cast iron skillet. Together, we walked out to my car.

We entered my house through the laundry room. Setting the box down just inside the door, I noted the washer was on its first spin cycle.

"Julie," I called. "Are you home?"

"Hey, Mom, I'm in here." Her voice echoed down the hallway, and I led my father to the den where Julie sat on the floor, her textbooks open before her on the coffee table.

Julie looked up as we entered. "*Buelito*," she said, standing to give him a hug.

"*Mijita*." He wrapped his arms around her, and I left them to catch up while I saw about dinner.

Only when I entered my contemporary kitchen, did I realize my refrigerator was nearly as empty as my father's. I searched the cupboards and found the only ingredients I had were those for chicken *flautas*. I considered going to the market, but did not wish to miss any time with my father and daughter. So, for the fourth time, I attempted the recipe.

I cooked quickly, not worrying about making my mother's *flautas*, but focusing instead on the expected pleasure of eating with my family. I used the tortillas from the store, rather than trying the press. I would do that when I had more time. Soon the flautas were ready, my husband was home, and Julie had set the square black table in the breakfast nook, even lighting the two silver tapers I usually left for show. My father was smiling at his granddaughter, and my heart felt lighter than it had in weeks.

I brought the *flautas* to the table, and my father served them as he did every time we ate at my parents' house.

"Oh goody," Julie said, slipping into her black and chrome chair. "I haven't had *flautas* in forever."

I felt a small catch in my throat, fearing her disappointment. She picked up a *flauta* and took a large bite. My father and husband did the same. Gripped by sudden fear, I sat frozen, studying the reflection of the candles off of the surface of the shiny black table.

Julie set down her *flauta*, and I looked up to meet her eyes.

"I'm sorry," I said before she could speak. "I know they are not *Buelita's flautas*."

Confusion crossed Julie's face, followed by understanding, followed by a smile.

"No, Mama," she said. "They are not." She looked at my father, and then my husband, and then back to me. "But," she said, her eyes warm and honest. "I think they are better."

About the Authors

Courtney Annicchiarico has lived in the Lehigh Valley for the past ten years with her loving husband, their two sons, and their crazy dog, Macs. When she is not writing, she knits badly, bakes, and works to raise Autism awareness.

Jeff Baird is a natural Redhead, a career educator at the secondary and post graduate level, and a self-proclaimed computer junkie. He has presented at numerous state and national technology conferences, and has published in the field of educational technology. He now turns his energies to publishing humorous memoirs about all things Redhead. He resides in the Lehigh Valley, Pennsylvania with his wife Mary, a Redhead wannabe, natural Redheaded children, Ashley and Ryan, and their dogs Casey and Bailey, both of them Honorary Redheads. You can find his collection of short stories, Redheaded Ruminations, on Amazon and his website at www.jeffbaird.net and find him on Facebook at: https://www.facebook.com/pages/Jeff-Baird-Redheads-Rule/126826860667586?fref=ts

Terrie Daugherty has lived in New Jersey, Connecticut, and Pennsylvania. She has been writing for most of her life and has poems and stories published in school and college papers and newsletters. She was a copy editor for *Once Around the Sun: Sweet, Funny, and Strange Tales for All Seasons,* and has been involved with several writer's groups. She works for a bank and fosters cats for a rescue organization. This is her first story published in an anthology.

A. E. Decker has been a member of the Bethlehem Writers Group since 2011. A former ESL tutor and doll-maker turned writer of fantasy, her short stories have appeared in such magazines as *Beneath Ceaseless Skies, Fireside Magazine,* and *The Sockdolager,* as well as in the BWG's own anthology, *Once Around the Sun,* which she helped edit. Her YA novel, *The Falling of the Moon,* was published by World Weaver Press in October 2015. Like all writers, she is owned by three cats.

BERNADETTE DE COURCEY was born and raised in Connemara, Ireland, where the Connemara Pony is still bred by her family. She graduated with an MA in Modern English Literature from the University of Limerick, Ireland, and currently teaches English as an online adjunct professor for Keiser University, while raising her two young sons. She is the co-editor of the literary e-zine *Bethlehem Writers Roundtable,* and has two stories published in the award-winning anthology *Once Around the Sun.* Recently she co-edited the eBook *Let it Snow* which is a collection of short stories available on Amazon.

It was suggested to **MARIANNE H. DONLEY,** when she was six, that she become a math teacher. Flush from the success of teaching her five-year-old sister how to add and subtract, this seemed like an excellent idea. After a few math classes, Marianne realized math teachers routinely lie to their students. Examples: You can't subtract a larger number from smaller number. You can't divide a smaller number by a larger number. When you multiply two numbers the product is always larger. She continued taking math courses because she figured she would eventually learn that you can divide by zero. While that never happened, she did teach mathematics to a variety of students from middle school to university level without ever lying to them. She now writes fiction from short stories to funny romances and quirky murder mysteries. She makes her home in Pennsylvania with her husband and a tank full of multiplying fish. She is a member of The Bethlehem Writers Group, Sisters in Crime, SinC Guppies, Romance Writers of America, Orange County Chapter/RWA, and Penn Jersey Women Writers Guild. You can find Marianne on social media at: www.facebook.com/mariannehdonley, www. mariannedonley.com, and https://twitter.com/mariannedonley

Tracy Falenwolfe was a stay-at-home mom for fifteen years before resurrecting her career in retail management and promptly deciding she had more fun in the fictional worlds of her own creation than she did at the mall. She lives in Pennsylvania's Lehigh Valley with her husband and two sons, where she's currently working on a mystery series. She also writes short stories and essays which she affectionately dubs her midlife crisis fiction. Her essay, "Love Me Do," appears in the *Unfinished Chapters* anthology available from Amazon. You can reach Tracy at tafwolfe@gmail.com.

Headley Hauser would stop carping about the monetary system if only some of the monetary would come his way. In the midst of his complaining, he has managed to write three novellas: *Trouble in Taos, Volition Man,* and *Dirk Destroyer's Less Destructive Brother,* all available as eBooks on Amazon. He also maintains the nearly popular, but entirely unprofitable blog, Just Plain Stupid at http://headleystupid.blogspot.com/. Headley lives, and does most of his whining, in Winston-Salem, NC.

Ralph Hieb enjoys reading and writing paranormal fiction. He resides in Bethlehem, Pennsylvania, with his wife Nancy. The couple enjoys travel, and makes a point each year to take a trip to someplace they have never seen before. In addition to being a member of the Bethlehem Writers Group, he is a member of the Greater Lehigh Valley Writers Group, where he has served as president and a member representative on the board of directors.

Jerry McFadden has been writing fiction for the past several years. His stories have appeared in various magazines and e-zines, such as *Flash Fiction Offensive, Over My Dead Body, Eclectic Flash Fiction*, and *Bethlehem Writers Roundtable*. He received a second place Bullet Award for the best crime fiction to appear on the web in June, 2011, and has had his short stories performed aloud on the stage by the Liar's League in London and the Liar's League in Hong Kong. His stories have also appeared in various anthologies, including *Hard Boiled Crime Scene, Deep Dark Woods, Once Around the Sun, A Christmas Sampler*, and *Let It Snow*.

GEOFFREY MEHL is a writer of fiction and nonfiction, a photographer, and a sustainable landscaping advocate who lives in northeastern Pennsylvania. He is the Author of *Stray Cats* (fiction), *A Gardener's Guide to Native Plants of Northeastern Pennsylvania* (non-fiction), and *Perennials—Habitat and Culture* (non-fiction). Avocational interests include publishing and graphic design, native plant gardening, and cooking and baking. His website is: www.geoffmehl.com, and Facebook at https://www.facebook.com/pages/Geoffrey-Mehl/1456580037997105

JUDITH MEHL's latest book, *Murder Most Floral*, follows two others in the Handwriting Analysis Mystery series: *Formula for Murder* and *Game, Set, Murder*. She is a veteran writer, handwriting analysis enthusiast, a gardener, and quilter. She is a member of the international group, American Association of Handwriting Analysts, plus quilting groups, and an herb club. Additionally, she is a member of Sisters in Crime, the Bethlehem Writer's Group, and Pocono Writers.

EMILY P. W. MURPHY is a writer and freelance editor. Her short stories appear in A *Christmas Sampler: Sweet, Funny, and Strange Holiday Tales* and in *Once Around the Sun: Sweet, Funny, and Strange Tales for All Seasons*, among other publications. After growing up in Pennsylvania, she has relocated to the Washington, DC area with her husband Adam, their two children, and their three cats. You can visit Emily's website at: http://www.emilypwmurphy.com.

SALLY W. PARADYSZ writes from the cabin she built in the woods in Bucks County, Pennsylvania, and works as a spiritual counselor. Her memoir, *From Scratch*, published in 2015, tells the story of building her house and rebuilding her life after the pains of sexual assault and a thirty-five year marriage ending in divorce. She won Honorable Mention for an inspirational story in the Writer's Digest 78th Annual Writing Competition in 2009. She was a finalist in the Salem (MA) Literary Festival in 2010, and published a non-fiction story in 11:11 Magazine. Her essay, "Tool-belt Spirituality" appears among those of such other authors as Gloria Steinem and Jimmy Carter in the collection *65 Things to Do When You Retire*, and her essay, "Just With Your Heart," appears in the anthology, *70 Things to Do When You Turn 70*. Her website can be found at http://sallyparadysz. com, and she blogs at Finding Paradysz in the Woods at http:// sallywparadyzs.blogspot.com

C. A. ROWLAND writes short stories in multiple genres and is currently finishing her first humorous amateur sleuth mystery novel set in Savannah, Georgia. Ms. Rowland is a member of the Virginia Writer's Club, Sisters-In-Crime, and Society of Children's Book Writers and Illustrators. Her official website and blog are at www.carowland.com and she is a regular blogger for www.mostlymystery.com.

E. L. RYAN was born and lives in Pennsylvania. He is a software developer and a creator of DraftMap editing software. This program helps writers identify and correct a variety of stylistic and grammatical issues in a manuscript, and is available at https://draftmap.com/. He writes a variety of fiction across several media, and enjoys hiking with his dog.

DIANE SISMOUR has written poetry and fiction for over 35 years in multiple genres. She lives with her husband in eastern Pennsylvania at the foothills of the Blue Mountains. Diane is a member of Romance Writers of America, Bethlehem Writer's Group LLC, Horror Writers Association, and Liberty States Fiction Writers. Her website is www.dianesismour.com, and her blog is www.dianesismour.blogspot.com. You can find her at Facebook and Twitter at: http://facebook.com/dianesismour, http://facebook.com/networkforthearts, https://twitter.com/dianesismour

PAUL WEIDKNECHT'S *work has appeared most recently in Agave Magazine, Appalachia, Best New Writing 2015, The Binnacle, The Comstock Review, Gray's Sporting Journal, The Hippocrates Prize for Poetry and Medicine* anthology, *The MacGuffin, Potomac Review,* and *Structo,* among others. He lives in Phillipsburg, New Jersey, where he has completed a collection of short fiction and is currently at work on a novel. He is a fan of the Boston Red Sox and Philadelphia Eagles, and he enjoys traveling, fly-fishing, and listening to '80s hair band music (yes, still).

CAROL L. WRIGHT is a recovering lawyer and academic who has traded writing on law-related topics for writing fiction. She has published several short stories in a variety of genres. Her upcoming "Gracie McIntyre Mysteries" series is set in the Berkshire foothills of Massachusetts. She is a life member of Sisters in Crime and the Jane Austen Society of North America, a member of SinC Guppies, and a founding member of the Bethlehem Writers Group. She is married to her college sweetheart, and lives in the Lehigh Valley of Pennsylvania. You can visit her website at: http://www.carollwright.com.

Acknowledgements

The Bethlehem Writers Group, LLC, would like to acknowledge the contributions of those who helped to make this book a reality.

We especially thank the esteemed authors Rebecca Forster and Curtis Smith. Ms. Forster served as the judge of the 2014 Bethlehem Writers Roundtable Short Story Award and selected "Preserves" by Tracy Falenwolfe as the first-place winner. Mr Smith served as the 2015 judge of the Short Story Award Competition. He selected "The History of a Fruitcake" by C. A. Rowland as the first-place winner. Both of these first-place stories appear in this compilation.

In addition, we thank BWG members Paul Weidknecht and Judith Mehl who gave valuable editorial assistance, and Diane Sismour who shared her artistic eye with our cover designer.

No book is ever produced without the cooperation of a large team of talented individuals, and we are most grateful to all those who dedicated countless hours to see this volume through to fruition.